Falling For Sharde

To order additional copies, please contact us.
BookSurge, LLC
www.booksurge.com
1-866-308-6235
orders@booksurge.com

Falling For Sharde

Marilyn Lee

2006

Falling For Sharde

CHAPTER ONE

She lay naked on her stomach with her legs parted, her eyes closed, and her hands spread on either side of her head. The man lying on top of her whispered against her ear, "You are so beautiful. . .so sexy. You feel so good .. so hot. . .so tight. . .so slick. I've never felt this way with anyone else. I can't get enough of you. . .I love you so much."

His words danced over her skin like a silken caress. A riot of emotions raced through her. She felt loved, desired, adored, and free to be as wanton as she'd always longed to be with him. "I love you too," she moaned. "I hunger for you. Feed my hunger. Fuck me!"

He laced his fingers through hers, kissed the back of her neck, lowered his powerful hips against her butt, and slowly, deliciously stroked his thick, hard length deep into the center of her slick need. The fire in her belly raged and spread lower, coming to an aching, burning stop between her legs.

Raining kisses onto her neck and filling her ears and heart with hot words of love and lust for her sensuous, dark body, he stroked deep and hard into her, branding her and claiming her body and her heart as his alone.

She had waited so long for these sweet, wonderful moments so full of passion and delight. A wave of need, love, and lust crashed over her. The fire in her core became a raging inferno, consuming her. Her body on fire, she cried out, shattering into a million, blissful, blazing pieces around his plundering cock.

"Oh, baby! Yes!" Nipping at her neck, he lowered his full weight onto her body, squeezing her hands so hard her fingers tingled. He thrust hard and deep. . .so deep her toes curled. Arching her back, she gasped with a combination of joy and pain as he came, filling her with his seed.

She lay smoldering under him, gasping with pleasure, her heart racing, savoring the knowledge that there was nothing between them. . .no inhibitions. . .no condoms. There was just their love and their desire for each other.

I

"I love you so much, Jefferson."

There was no response and in a moment, his big, hard body no longer pressed down on hers. She turned, opened her eyes, and groaned—as the dream faded.

Sharde Donovan lay alone in her bed, her nightgown soaked, her panties damp, and her heart aching. She turned and buried her face in her pillow, bitter tears stinging her eyes. She could not go on like this. Something had to give. Either she had to find a way to catch Jefferson Calder's eye, or she had to make a clean break and move on with her life.

That would mean leaving her job as Technology Manager at Calder Technologies. She'd been with the company for nine years. She loved her job, but her increasingly graphic and erotic dreams were a sign she was but a breath away from becoming obsessed with a man who saw her as nothing more than his efficient technology manager/confidant. As things stood now, she had absolutely no chance of ever becoming the woman Jefferson sought out when he wanted to make love. Calder's woman. That's what she longed to be. During the nine years she'd known him, she'd dated and been intimate with a few men, but always found herself comparing each lover to Jefferson. She sighed. Small wonder none of her relationships had blossomed into anything lasting or worthwhile.

She rolled onto her back and slid out of bed. She walked into the bathroom, tossed her nightgown and panties into the hamper, and stared at her reflection in the medicine cabinet mirror. Bare of make up, the face that stared back at her was golden brown and smooth. Her lips were full, her eyes hazel. With make up and a little help from complimentary lighting, she suspected some men might consider her "cute," but far from pretty.

Cute women didn't land hunks like Jefferson. Gorgeous men like him ended up with the sexy, sultry women uninhibited enough to make the most of their sexuality to get what they wanted. While she had no desire to slink around collecting men like trophies, she did want Jefferson. The question was how much she wanted him and what was she prepared to do to get him.

She sighed and walked to the shower. She stood under the cool water. *Okay, Sharde. Playtime is over. You have one month to turn his head. One month. If he doesn't notice you're a blasted woman within that time, you give your notice and you walk away. And you don't look back.*

Her thoughts drifted to the last time she'd been alone with him, two weeks earlier. She tightened her lips. *You're not spending another blasted Super Bowl Sunday with him being treated like one of the boys. And there will be no more "dates" that aren't dates. When March Madness rolls around, if he hasn't shaped up by then, he can get another "boy" to sit and watch all those college basketball games with him!*

***

As she drove to work that morning, the dull, gray sky mirrored her mood. When she stepped out of her car, a chill wind slapped her in the face. February was definitely not one of her favorite months—especially not in Philly. If not for her obsession with Jefferson, she'd have packed her bags after gaining a few years of experience and headed for a warmer climate after graduating from Temple University.

She pulled her coat closer around her neck and hurried into the building. Fifteen minutes later, she encountered Jefferson in the coffee room. As it nearly always did, her heart hammered in her chest and her mouth went dry at the sight of him.

"'Morning, Sharde." His brief smile didn't quite reach his smoky gray eyes and he walked out of the room without giving her a chance to do more than mutter "morning" in return.

And he certainly hadn't noticed the expensive new dress she

wore. *That went well*, she thought as she headed back to her office. *He'll be falling at your feet in no time.*

"'Morning, Sharde."

She paused at her open office door. A tall, voluptuous woman with beautiful dark eyes, deep, gorgeous mocha skin, and a beauty to rival former Miss America Vanessa Williams, came to meet her. Although far from super model thin, Darbi Raymond made every ounce work for her, carrying herself with an air that seemed to suggest full-figured women had more fun.

If Jefferson was going to date a black woman who had neither Vanessa Williams' beauty or her size, surely it would be someone as breathtakingly beautiful as Darbi rather than someone "cute" and a little on the chubby side like herself.

Sharde stifled a sigh. Being in love was the pits. She'd always had what her mother called "meat on her bones," but had never worried about it until she realized Jefferson went in for pole-thin, super gorgeous women like his ex, and maybe Darbi. Yet, as far as she knew, Jefferson had never given Darbi a second glance nor had he shown any interest in spending any of his free time with her.

On the other hand, he and Sharde spent so much of their free time together they had keys to each other's places. And he depended on her, as well as trusted her judgment. Surely getting him to see her as a desirable woman couldn't be that hard now that she'd given herself a deadline.

"Hey. Anyone in there?"

Realizing she'd allowed her thoughts to wander, she smiled. "Good morning, Darbi." Noting the cup in the other woman's hand, she gestured toward her office. "Join me?"

Darbi nodded and followed her into her office.

Although she and Darbi had grown up in the same neighborhood and gone to the same schools, it was only after she'd hired Darbi to be her assistant three years earlier, that they became close friends. Darbi admired how Sharde had worked her way through college and into the number two position at Calder Technologies, a multi-million dollar electronics company, in nine years. While admiring Darbi's work ethics, Sharde was in awe of how any woman as beautiful as Darbi could shake off a painful, unwanted divorce and embrace what she called her second virginity with such single-mindedness.

The only thing Sharde wanted to embrace was Jefferson. Of course, she wanted to do more than embrace him. A smile curved her lips. She wanted to do a lot more than hug him. Lord, that man's sheer masculinity filled her heart and head with lustful thoughts of incredible magnitude.

"And just what are you thinking that makes you smile like the cat that caught the last tasty rodent?"

Sharde grinned. "Girl, if you only knew!"

Darbi's smile invited her confidence. "So tell me."

But she wasn't ready to admit even to Darbi that she had a thing for Jefferson. She shook her head. "I was just thinking how much...I need some intimacy."

Darbi sighed. "Believe me, I know the feeling only too well."

She sat back in her chair, studying Darbi. "How long has it been for you?"

Darbi sipped her coffee. "Nearly three years."

"Don't you...miss sex?"

"Sometimes." She shrugged. "Okay, a lot, but I'm thirty-two now and I no longer want sex for sex's sake. I want commitment and marriage with the sex. Sex without those no longer holds any appeal for me."

Sharde sighed. She wanted commitment and marriage as well, but she had a feeling that if given the chance, she would take sex for its own sake with Jefferson. "I might get there one day, but I'm not there yet."

"Well, it took a broken marriage and two other headaches to get me where I am now. Hopefully you can get what you want without getting stung as I have."

The desire to admit her feelings for Jefferson was difficult to overcome. She sighed again and they drank their coffee in silence, each lost in her own thoughts.

Later that morning, Sharde sat in her office, frowning at her computer monitor while she discarded plan after plan for capturing Jefferson's heart. Failing that, she'd settle for being the object of his lust.

Her thoughts turned to their coffee room encounter. Fat chance she had of that happening. Probably, if she walked into his office stark naked, he'd give her a puzzled look and ask if she'd done something different with her hair!

"To hell with this!"

She looked up. Her half-open office door swung wide and Jefferson stalked inside. Her heart thumped in her chest. Talk about eye candy. He was tall, well-built, and drop-dead gorgeous. His hair was short and dark, his eyes an intense gray.

She immediately saw he was annoyed. But even that didn't distract from his breathtaking looks. Lord, she'd never seen such a sexy man. Just looking at him fully clothed and completely unaware of her as a woman made her wet and hungry for him.

"What's up, Jefferson?" As she spoke, she ate him up with her eyes. She drank in the power inherent in his big, muscular body. He stalked the length of her office with all the grace of a sleek, predatory cat on the prowl. Finally he leaned across her desk and looked into her eyes. "I'm feeling wound up and horny as hell. I'm going to the cabin for a few days."

He had a deep, warm baritone that sent a shiver of longing

through her every time he spoke. And it was time she heard that sweet baritone whispering something sexually exciting and suggestive in her ear.

"Great idea." She smiled. "I wish I could join you. I could use a few days of peace and quiet. I'm feeling a little wound up myself."

He considered her in silence, one brow arched. Just as she thought he was about to say he wanted to be alone, he shrugged. "So come with me."

Just for a moment, Sharde thought she had died and gone to heaven. After years of watching him eat his heart out, first for his faithless ex-wife and then for his equally faithless ex-fiancée, she was finally about to get a chance to make sure he saw the forest for the trees—her.

"Ben out of town again?" she asked of his best friend.

He nodded. "But even if he wasn't, I'm not in the mood for his company. I'd rather you came."

"There's only one bedroom," she pointed out.

He grinned. "We can share it."

Her heart thudded. Her spirits soared. She swallowed painfully, going wet at the thought of spending a long weekend at the remote cabin he owned in New York State with a wound up and horny Jefferson. Lord, but she'd give anything to love all his frustrations away.

"Share it?"

His eyes held no trace of lust. Horny he might be, but she was not on his sexual radar. Hell. He was never going to be horny for her unless she did something to make him notice her as a woman.

Almost as if he'd read her mind and wanted to make it clear why he wanted her company, he straightened and thrust his hands in his pockets. "Okay, I guess that wouldn't be very practical. I'll bring my sleeping bag and use that in the living room. You can have the bedroom."

He'd sleep in his sleeping bag alone when hell froze over.

He looked at her. "We can go bar hopping together and you can stop me from picking up some beautiful blonde bimbo in a bar and falling for her."

Both his ex-wife and his ex-fiancée were blondes. Why couldn't he expand his horizons and see the tall, shapely, albeit none-too-thin, black woman waiting to rock his world? She feared she had little chance of ever getting him hot and horny—unless she got him drunk first. And that was out of the question. He would have to accept her just as she was—sober—or she was wasting her time. "Isn't that what men want when they're horny?"

He shrugged. "I've had it with women and committed relationships. I just want sex with no commitments offered or expected."

He wasn't making any sense and she understood why. After three years of marriage, he had walked in on his wife, Linda, with another man. Sharde had watched him shy away from women for two years after his divorce.

Sharde had been with him through his divorce and the tough two years following it, but when he was ready to date again, he had looked elsewhere for love. She'd been dating someone at the time, but she knew that hadn't made any difference. He was just too used to thinking of her as a friend to envision her as a lover.

Nine and a half months earlier, he had asked her to accompany him to a charity function where he met Vanessa Del Warren. Sharde had watched in dismay as the beautiful blonde had taken one look at him, smiled, cast out her line, and easily reeled him in.

He had sent Sharde home in a cab. Although she and he had plans to work on the office budget that weekend, she had not seen or heard from him again. He arrived at work late Monday morning. Later that day, Vanessa Del Warren had waltzed into the office to show off the expensive engagement ring Jefferson had bought her that morning.

Although Jefferson had been eager to get married, he had confessed to Sharde that Vanessa was in no hurry to tie the knot. When Calder Technologies failed to win a multi-million dollar government contract, Vanessa had left him to pursue Clayton Frazier, the owner of Fra-Tech, the company with the winning bid. Admittedly Clayton Frazier was drop-dead, panty-wetting gorgeous, but then, so was Jefferson.

Two selfish bimbo bitches had hurt and jaded him, making it harder for a woman who really loved him to win his heart.

She sighed, pushing the memories away. "Not all women are faithless, Jefferson."

His gaze narrowed. "Maybe not, but the ones who aren't leave me cold."

She felt as if he'd tossed a bucket of ice water on her. It was hopeless. He would never see her as a woman capable of fulfilling his sexual fantasies and desires. "I think I'll pass on coming to the cabin after all."

He frowned. "Why?"

Because I'm tired of breaking my heart over you, you big, blind ox! She glanced at her computer. "If we're going to have a hope of landing that next government contract, we're going to need to have more staff in place and I'm still sifting through résumés for new analysts and—"

"Darbi is perfectly capable of sifting through them and flagging the most promising ones for your attention. We hired her to help secure new contracts and lighten your burden. Let her do her job."

In the three years that Darbi had worked for the company, she had become invaluable to Sharde, not only assisting in the everyday running of the company, but doing most of the travel, freeing both Sharde and Jefferson to concentrate on overseeing design and development of new technologies.

She nodded. "I guess you're right. Hiring her was one of our best personnel moves in years. She doesn't mind all the traveling, she's a hard worker, and she gets the job done right the first time."

"So let her do it."

She sat back in her seat. "And she's stunningly beautiful. Don't you think so?"

He shrugged. "Yes. So how about you allow the stunningly beautiful Darbi to do what she was hired to do? Take the pressure off you, which will leave you free to come with me. Suddenly the thought of being there alone doesn't appeal."

So he had noticed how beautiful Darbi was! Just how much else had he noticed? "Would you like to ask her to accompany you?"

He arched a brow. "What? Why the hell would I want her to come with me?"

"She's beautiful. . .you just said so."

"So? She's not my type."

"Maybe if you got to know her, you'd find she is."

He leaned across her desk and stared into her eyes. "Let me make myself crystal clear, Sharde, I have absolutely no personal interest in Darbi. Is that clear enough for you?"

"Why not? Is it because she's black?"

"It's because she doesn't interest me—period!" His eyes narrowed. "Her skin color is not a factor. Contrary to what you might think you know about men, not every man is a sucker for a beautiful woman."

"So if she were a white blonde—"

"What is it with you and this harping on race?"

"I'm not harping on it. I'm just curious."

"Really? Well, although I admit to having a special fondness for blondes, I have dated women who were neither blonde nor white. If a woman interests me, the color of her skin or hair is not a major issue for me. So don't go there, Sharde."

Feeling an invisible weight lift off her shoulders, she sat back in her seat, a small smile curving her lips. Her half-formed fear that he was not attracted to black women had been unfounded. She frowned. But then he had said it was not a major issue. Did that mean it was an issue for him—even if only a minor one?

"Sharde?"

She flashed a quick smile at him. "So, when do you want to head out for the cabin?"

"Did you really think color is an issue with me, Sharde?"

She saw the concern in his eyes and shook her head. "Not in a bad way, Jeff." She shrugged. "But it would be normal for you to prefer white women."

"Would it? Have you always dated black men?"

"Mostly, yes. Although in high school, I had this monumental crush on Ricardo Montalban." She gave a gusty sigh. "The fantasies the man starred in my head would probably make him blush."

He smiled. "Since we're sharing secrets, I used to lie awake at night suffering big time lust for Eartha Kitt. I can't tell you how many cold showers I took on her behalf. I always wanted to play Batman to her Catwoman."

She leaned forward, put her face close to his, and purred.

He smiled, then sighed. "You know, no matter how bad things are, you have a way of making them seen better for me. I don't know what I would have done without you at my side these last few years."

The words, spoken in a low, sincere voice held little comfort. She was long past the point where she wanted to be his rock. Being the woman he turned to when he wanted to get physical was more important to her these days. She suppressed a sigh and forced a smile. "You'd have been fine. Ben would have seen to that."

"Benton is the best friend a man could have…" He touched her cheek. "But sometimes a man needs or wants a woman's perspective."

"A woman…that's me," she said softly.

He nodded. "I know."

But she doubted that. "We're leaving when?"

"We can go this afternoon. We'll make a long weekend of it and come back Monday night."

Four days and three nights spent alone with him in a small, remote cabin. She moistened her lips. "It might snow."

He shrugged. "I'll leave now and get everything we'll need for a few days. All you'll need to do is pack warm clothing and several books. I'll pick you up at your place at three and we'll get there in time for dinner. Okay?"

That would give her several hours to devise a plan for ending up in his bed before the weekend was over. She nodded. "Okay."

"Great." He smiled and her heart jumped in her chest. "I'll see you in a few hours."

"Okay."

***

Twenty minutes later, seated in one of the leather chairs in front of Sharde's desk, Darbi studied her face. "You're spending a long weekend with the boss?"

Noting Darbi's lack of surprise, Sharde sighed. "You don't sound surprised."

Darbi shrugged. "I can't say I am. I've suspected for some time that there's more than friendship between you two."

Sharde blinked. "You have? Why?"

She shrugged. "It has something to do with the way you look at him and the sound of his voice when he's talking to or about you. You look at him like a woman looks at a special lover and his voice always softens when he talks about you."

Sharde shook her head slowly. She could believe that her feelings for Jefferson were not always concealed, but she'd never noticed any softening of his voice when he spoke to her. "I'm not sure what you are seeing or hearing, but there's nothing between us. We're friends."

"With benefits?"

Friends with benefits. That described the only way she'd be interested in remaining friends with him. "No. Just friends."

"So this weekend. . .you're hoping to change that?"

She shrugged. "Do you think it's possible?"

"I'm surprised it's not already true. The passion simmering just under the surface between you two seems explosive."

"Don't I wish." She shook her head. "Back to business. You'll be all right until Tuesday?"

"Of course. What about you? Are you going to be all right on Tuesday?"

"I'll be fine. . .no matter what the weekend brings or doesn't bring. Either way, it's time I took control of my own happiness again."

"If you want to talk. . ."

She shook her head. "This is something I need to work out in my own mind first. But thanks, Darbi."

Darbi smiled. "That's what friends are for. So I'll see you on Tuesday."

***

Ninety minutes into the three-hour drive, snow fell hard and heavy, making driving and visibility difficult. Sharde sat in the passenger seat of Jefferson's SUV, praying he wouldn't decide to turn around and head home. No matter what, if they made it to the cabin, she was going to find a way to get him in bed before the weekend was over.

Five hours after they'd left Philly, he stopped the SUV in front of the cabin. They sat staring through the windshield. Several inches of snow covered the roof and the ground around the small cabin. The snow still fell heavily. She squinted. Or was it now sleet?

He swore softly and reached into the glove compartment for a flashlight. "I'd better go see how things stand. Wait here," he told her and climbed out of the vehicle, leaving the engine running.

She cast a smile upward, leaned back against her seat, and offered a silent prayer of thanksgiving. The weather had done its part, now she had to do hers. She closed her eyes, considering strategies for seducing him.

"Damn!"

The harsh sound and a cold blast of air snapped Sharde out of her lovely thoughts of nights of lust and unbridled passion spent under Jefferson's big, sweaty, thrusting body.

Cheeks hot, she opened her eyes. Jefferson slid into the driver's seat.

"So?"

"The power is out and it's cold as hell out there and inside. We'll be snowed in if this damn snow doesn't stop soon."

A feeling of delight danced through her. It was difficult not to laugh out loud or at least grin. She cast a quick glance upwards. Someone up there must think it was time to give her a chance at happiness…or a taste of bliss, Calder style.

"There's a fireplace in the cabin," she reminded him. She went hot and then cold at the thought of lying naked and aroused in front of a roaring fire with Jefferson lying on top of her, between her legs, loving away all her emotional aches and pains.

He squinted through the windshield. "Maybe we should go back now while we still can."

She fought back panic. "It took five hours to get here. God only knows how long it would take to get back. Why don't we just go inside, start a fire, and get something to eat? I'm tired and hungry." *And desperate to be alone and snowbound with you.*

He sighed. "Okay."

She released her seatbelt and moved to open her door.

His arm brushed against her breasts as he reached across her to place a hand on hers over the door handle. "It's cold as hell and slippery out there. Stay here while I start a fire and get our stuff inside."

Very aware of his arm brushing against her body, she turned her head. His gray eyes were inches away. "It will go faster if I help carry our bags inside."

"Stay inside," he said again, withdrew his arm, and got out.

Enjoying the warmth of the SUV, she watched him make several trips to the cabin. She had seen how chivalrous he could be when he was in love, but he'd always tended to treat her like an old family friend instead of a woman he wanted or needed to play Sir Galahad with. It was nice to have him behaved that way with her. A smile touched her lips.

Fifteen minutes later, he emerged from the cabin and opened her door. She turned off the engine, removed the keys, and was surprised when he placed his hands on her waist and lifted her down.

She smiled at him. "Thanks."

"Be careful," he said and turned away.

She took a step, her right foot landed on a slick patch of snow and slid out from under her. "Jefferson!"

He whirled around, slightly off balance, his arm shooting around her waist. "It's all right. I've got you," he said against her forehead.

Heart hammering, she sighed and leaned against him, laughing weakly. "That was close."

"Too close. I told you it was slippery as hell out here." He took a step back to balance himself. His foot hit a slick patch. He made a small sound of surprise, his arm tightened around her waist, and he lost his balance.

She tried to steady him, but he was too heavy. He fell, taking her with him. He slammed onto the snow with her on top of him. "Damn! What more could possibly go wrong?" he demanded furiously.

From where Sharde lay, sprawled between his legs, things were perfect. She lifted her head and looked down into his eyes, laughing.

He frowned. "Exactly what amuses you about our present situation?"

Her smile widened. "You're awfully cute sprawled in the snow like a six-foot plus snowman."

His eyes danced with amusement and he laughed. "You're nuts, Sharde."

"Yes," she admitted, softening her voice. "About you."

"Same here, toots."

"No." She touched his face. "I really meant that," she whispered.

He arched a brow. "So did I. You know I'm nuts about you."

To her delight, he clamped a hand on the back of her head, brought her mouth down to his, and brushed his lips against hers.

At least, she later decided he'd only intended to brush his mouth against hers. But not one to waste opportunities, she parted her lips, touched the tip of her tongue to his, and planted a long, moist, hungry kiss against his mouth.

He stiffened under her, his hands moving up to push against her shoulders.

Determined to make the most of this unexpected opportunity, Sharde pressed closer between his legs, thrusting her groin against his, and deepened the kiss. She greedily sucked his tongue between her lips and into her mouth.

As he shuddered against her, she kissed him slowly, deeply—again and again, tasting the surprising sweetness of his lips and the moist heat of his tongue. She poured all her pent up desire and hunger for him into the demanding kisses, trying to overwhelm his senses. She kept her lips pressed tight and close to his, not giving either of them a chance to take a deep breath between kisses. Within moments, his lips moved against hers and his hands slid from her shoulders to her back to hold her close. Only then did she move her mouth away from his so she could rain a series of warm, nibbling kisses against his face.

"Jeff..."

He sucked in a deep, gasping breath. "Sharde! What the hell are you doing?"

His voice came out brusque and low.

A smile curved her lips. She finally had his attention. She curled her fingers in his hair and stared down into his eyes. "Thanking you for saving me from a nasty fall."

"By kissing me until I hardly know who I am?"

"Hey! Is it my fault you have such sweet, luscious, kissable lips?"

"What?"

She bent her head and sensuously outlined his mouth with the tip of her tongue. "Hmmm. Your lips are warm and they taste sweeter than wine. A woman could get a natural high from kissing you alone."

"Sharde—"

"Shhh. Talking now is not in my game plan, handsome." She slowly licked his lips before finally pressing a last long kiss against his mouth. "Thank you."

He stared up at her, his eyes almost black.

The silence between them stretched on for several moments, during which time neither of them moved. Then, without any warning, he rolled them over. When they came to a stop, she lay on her back in the snow with him between her legs.

He was aroused. She could feel the unmistakable bulge pressing against her. The breath caught in her throat and her heart hammered so wildly she could barely breathe. With the snowing pelting down, stinging her face, she stared up at him, her lips parted, her arms holding him close.

"Jeff..." she whispered his name, her voice clearly conveying her raw need. She slid a hand down to cup his buns.

"What the hell do you think you're doing, Sharde?"

"Isn't it obvious?"

His eyes narrowed. When he spoke, his tone shattered any

illusions she'd been nursing about him sharing her feelings. "You think I want to play house with you?"

The anger in his voice cooled her ardor. "You're aroused," she whispered.

"I'm human, but that doesn't change the fact that you've clearly taken leave of your senses!"

Her mouth worked, but no words emerged.

He pulled away and exploded to his feet.

She stared up at him, disappointment and hurt rushing through her. She'd overcome her natural inhibitions and thrown herself at him only to discover he didn't want her. Tears stung her eyes and tightened her throat.

He reached down, took her hands, and pulled her to her feet. Without waiting to see if she followed, he turned and made his way to the cabin.

She brushed the snow off her clothes. Taking a deep, shuddering breath, she wrapped her arms around her body. Maybe that would keep the hurt tucked away inside her. If she managed that, she could pretend he hadn't just ripped her heart from her body and tossed it into the snow like so much refuse.

She closed her eyes and turned her face towards the sky, relishing the sting of sleet striking her skin. He'd made his lack of interest in her ultra clear. Now what was she supposed to do?

"Sharde?" A hand descended on her shoulder.

She shook it off and slowly turned to face him. "I'll sleep in the SUV."

"Don't be ridiculous. You'd freeze."

"Then you sleep there."

"Do I look like I'm interested in freezing to death?" He closed his hands over her arms. "It's too cold to hold this conversation out here. Come inside where we can talk without danger of freezing to death."

"Why don't you go taking a flying leap?"

"What?"

"To hell with you!" She shook his hands off again and walked towards the open cabin door.

CHAPTER TWO

Jefferson watched Sharde walk towards the cabin, slipping and sliding every step of the way. He tensed several times, certain he'd have to risk life and limb sprinting across the slippery snow in an attempt to keep her from falling. He released a breath when she finally made her way into the cabin.

She slammed the door shut. Shaken by what had just happened between them and still aroused, he stood in the sleet. What the hell had possessed Sharde to kiss him with enough passion to get him rock hard? He breathed deeply, running his tongue along his mouth. Hell, he could still taste her hot, demanding lips devouring his mouth.

Who knew she could kiss like that? In the nine years they'd known each other, they'd spent several holidays together before his marriage and after his divorce. During those holidays, they'd exchanged gifts and light brushes of the lips, but they'd never actually locked lips. But damn, she knew how to arouse his passions and make him long for more than just kisses.

He licked his lips again. She'd been many things to him—office assistant, technology manager, a sounding board, and finally a confidant and friend. He had come to depend upon her levelheaded advice when things went wrong in his personal or professional life. She had never let him down or asked anything of him—until they'd sprawled together in the snow.

Although she had personal knowledge of all his romantic entanglements of the last few years, he knew very little of her love life. He hadn't heard her mention a man or a date in a very long time. He frowned. That probably explained what had just happened. Hell, even levelheaded confidants had needs. She'd just shared one of hers and he'd thoughtlessly rebuffed her. Damn, he was a selfish bastard.

He glanced towards the cabin. He'd needlessly hurt a woman who had been there for him when the two women he'd given his heart to had ripped it into little pieces and tossed it back at him. If she needed sex for sex's sake, how could he deny her? He recalled the taste of her lips moving hungrily over his. Who was he kidding? Sleeping with her would not be a sacrifice on his part. Any woman capable of putting that amount of heat into a few kisses would be dynamite in bed.

Thoughts of sleeping with Sharde for her sake gave way to a lust for satisfaction for its own sake. After he apologized, he'd need to find a way to get her into his bed. He turned and walked toward the cabin.

He went inside, closing the door on the cold, biting sleet. The interior of the cabin consisted of a large living room with a small kitchen to the right. Two doors dotted one wall of the living room. One door led to a small bathroom, the other to a medium-sized bedroom. With the power off, the fire he'd built in the fireplace provided the only heat. Several kerosene lamps illuminated the interior. He looked towards the kitchen—empty.

He hesitated, then shrugged, and walked towards the bedroom door. Silence greeted his tap. He raised his hand to knock again just as the door opened. Sharde stood in front of him.

In the office, she always wore her hair in an unassuming bun. Now it hung around her shoulders in a dark cloud, framing her smooth, brown face. He blinked. Her dark eyes, usually so sedate, sparkled with defiance, making the face he'd always considered just this side of plain look radiant and almost pretty. Almost?

"I suppose you expect me to explain or apologize for kissing you." She lifted her chin. "Well, I don't plan to do either. It happened. Deal with it." She pushed past him and walked towards the kitchen.

He turned to stare after her. He'd never seen this facet of her character. He tossed his gloves and coat onto the living room sofa and followed her into the kitchen. He leaned against the wall, watching as she unpacked the groceries he'd bought.

She turned to face him. "What?"

He shrugged, slipping his hands into his trouser pockets. "Actually, I wanted to apologize. I think you misunderstood what I said—"

"No, I didn't. You made your lack of interest exceedingly clear. I got the message, so don't worry."

He stared at her, intrigued. Where had this fascinating woman been hiding the last nine years? "We've always been able to talk about anything, Sharde. Let's not start building walls now."

She turned the propane-powered hotplate on before looking at him again, a weary look in her eyes. "What is there to discuss? I lost my head for a few moments and—"

"And so did I. And you know what, Sharde? I'd like it to happen again…if you're still willing."

She turned away from him and began seasoning two steaks. Noting how her hands shook, he straightened and walked over to her. He turned her to face him. "Are you seeing anyone?"

She shook her head.

He clasped her hands in his, bringing them to rest against his chest. "You know I'm not either, but the interlude in the snow is ample proof that we both have needs that aren't being met."

She looked up at him, her eyes wide and dark. "What's your point, Jeff?"

"That we should help each other during this dry period." She frowned and he changed gears. "Or at least for this week-end."

"Are you saying we should become lovers for the week-end?"

Her voice was low and breathy. Imagining how it would sound moaning in his ear as they had sex, made him hard. "It's a long weekend and we'll no doubt be stranded here for the next few days. We have to do something to pass the time."

"What?" She jerked away from him.

Smooth. Very smooth, Calder. That was one of the dumbest things you've ever said to a woman. "That came out all wrong."

"Did it?"

He closed his eyes briefly. Damn, if she was going to start challenging everything he said, she'd make him nuts. "Yes! I didn't mean it like it sounded."

She went back to the steaks. He watched her stab seasoning slits into the steak with little regard for the fact that she was in danger of mangling the expensive meat.

She flung the steaks into the barely warm frying pan, chopped huge hunks of onions and peppers on top, and turned to face him, the knife still in her hand. "Fine."

He blinked at her. "What?"

"I said fine."

"I heard what you said. But what did you mean?"

"What do you think I mean?"

"You want to sleep with me?"

She lifted her chin, a hint of rose staining her cheeks. Strange how he'd never noticed that she blushed so charmingly.

Her eyes sparkled like dark, beautiful jewels. "Not necessarily you, but with a man...yes."

He tightened his lips. "Are you saying any man would do?" He'd never given her love life much consideration, but now the thought of her sleeping around didn't sit well with him.

"Wouldn't any woman do for you?"

"No, any woman would not do. I don't sleep with just any-one in a dress."

She smiled, revealing an enchanting dimple in her right cheek. "Then isn't it lucky I'm wearing pants?"

He stared at her in amazement. How had he never realized how interesting she was? She took him from lust to anger right back to burning lust in a matter of moments. The next few days were going to be a journey of discovery. He planned to enjoy every moment of them.

She put the knife down and walked over to him. Placing her hands against his chest, she leaned into him and pressed a long, satisfying kiss against his mouth. She kissed him with a hunger that sent his cock rapidly expanding along the side of one leg.

He breathed in deeply, inhaling the passion and sweetness of her kiss. She slipped her arms around his neck. He held her close, savoring the lush warmth of her lips. Her body turned to liquid heat. She poured herself into his arms, molding her soft curves against him.

She rubbed against his groin and he nearly lost it. During the last few months of their relationship, Vanessa had been cold. It had been months since he'd been intimate, and he ached for sex.

He stroked his hands over her shoulders and down her back to her waist. Still savoring the hunger of her kisses, he slid his hands under her bulky sweatshirt. He moved his hands up her back and encountered something skimpy and lacey.

His questing hands moved over her back, searching for the clasp. After several attempts, he realized the bra must fasten in the front. Dragging his lips away from hers, he stepped back, reaching for the bottom of the baggy sweatshirt.

She shook her head and stepped away from him. "I'll take it off in front of the fire."

He cast a quick glance at the frying pan. "What about the meat?"

She turned the fire off and covered the frying pan. When she looked at him, he saw pure liquid lust in her dark gaze. She unzipped his pants. He shuddered as her long, soft fingers found the slit in his briefs and curled around his cock. "Right now I have a taste and need for another kind of meat. Fuck me?"

In all the time he'd known her, he'd never heard her so much as use hell or damn before that night. To hear her call his cock meat and ask him to fuck her turned him on big time. She was an enigma, a lady when needed, but a woman in the bedroom. "Oh, hell, yeah!"

She released him and walked to the living room area to stand in front of the fire. He moved across the room to the sofa. He had tossed his sleeping bag and two blankets behind it. He picked them up and spread them out on the floor, several feet from the fire. He turned to face her.

Locking his gaze with hers, he pulled off his sweater and tossed it near the sofa. She put a forefinger between her sweet lips and sucked it as she watched. His shirt and tee shirt followed. He found her sucking sexually suggestive and highly erotic. He loved that her lovely dark eyes seem to ravish his body as he bared his chest. He sat down to remove his boots and socks. He rose and reached for the waistband of his jeans.

She removed her finger from her mouth. "Let me."

A jolt of lust danced through him as he contemplated what she had in mind. The last time a woman had removed his pants, she'd given him a scorching balls suck, stopping just short of blowing him. He dropped his hands to his side. "Please do."

She removed her short boots and socks. He looked at her feet. Her toenails were unpolished, her feet nicely shaped and free of any oddities that would turn him off. He licked his lips. He'd love to start at her pretty feet and kiss his way up her body, stopping for an extended feast at her pussy before claiming her lips, sliding his aching cock deep inside her, and fucking her.

He shuddered. He hadn't even seen her body, but he was already so hot and hard he felt ready to explode. He hadn't been this horny for a woman he'd never seen fully naked since…hell, he'd never been this horny for a woman he'd never seen naked. He'd had a brief glimpse of her breasts a year earlier, but that memory paled in comparison to what he was about to see.

She placed her hands against his shoulders and moved her mouth over his chest, kissing and licking, making the light coating of hair on his chest stand on end.

Her lips felt soft and warm against his skin. Her mouth brushed against his right nipple. Hmmm. That felt nice? She touched her lips to his other nipple. Hmmm. She blew softly on his skin, the tip of her tongue sweeping over his nipple.

Oh, hell. Now there was no doubt. That felt good. "Oh, yeah," he said softly.

"If you like that. How about this?" She settled her lips over his right nipple and began to suck. A shock of pleasure shot through him. Holy hell! He clasped his hands over the back of her head, holding her mouth over his nipple, amazed it was so sensitive to pleasure.

She alternated sucking, licking, and biting each nipple until he gasped, shuddered, curled his fingers in her hair, and pulled away from her mouth. "You keep that up and you'll make me come too soon."

She gave him a lecherous smile, sliding the tip of her tongue over her full, sweet lips. "I'm going to do all kinds of wonderful things to you. My goal is for you to come early and often."

"Holy hell, Sharde, don't make me come too soon. I want to enjoy this."

"Oh, you'll enjoy it, all right. I promise."

He swallowed and released her hair.

Tongue extended, she pressed a parting kiss against each nipple. She then kissed her way down his body, over his abs. She dropped to her knees and looked up at him. Her dark eyes danced with desire and made him weak with longing.

"Now the fun begins." Pressing her lips against his lower abs, she unbuttoned his jeans. They were already unzipped. She placed her hands inside, pushing the jeans over his hips. The front of the material brushed against his erection and he groaned.

"If you keep this up much longer, you're going to make me come."

"Oh, you're definitely going to be coming, Jeff," she teased. With the jeans just above his knees, she leaned forward and lightly sank her teeth into his briefs, biting into his cock.

"Holy hell, Sharde!" He curled his fingers in her hair and gritted his teeth in an effort to hold back the explosion threatening to erupt from his cock. "Stop torturing me."

She removed her mouth and smiled up at him. "The best is yet to come."

"Oh, honey, I can't take much more of this without coming."

She reached into his briefs to cup his balls in her hand. He shuddered. He loved having a woman hold and touch his balls and cock.

"Hold on, handsome."

"Handsome?"

She pushed his jeans the rest of the way down his body and he stepped out of them. She tossed them away and smiled up at him. "You must know you're handsome, Jeff."

He knew women generally found him attractive. But handsome? He wasn't certain about that. Even if it were true, it hadn't done him much good in love.

She rose and stepped back to look at him. He stood before her with his cock and balls straining against his briefs. He was so hungry to slide into her he was on the verge of begging.

"You are such a hunk and for tonight...this weekend... you're all mine." She closed the distance between them and dropped to her knees. She kissed the bulge in his briefs and then breathing nosily, she quickly pushed his briefs over his hips, stopping with them just below his buns.

His aching length, fully erect, sprang forth and bounced in front of his body, hard and leaking from the tip.

She looked up at him, her eyes wide and lustful. "Oooh... my...oh, Jefferson...what a lovely, luscious piece of meat."

His heart hammered, making him almost breathless. "Would you like to taste me?"

"Yes!"

He quickly removed his briefs and stood naked, fully aroused and hungry before her. "It's all yours. Take as much of it into your mouth as you like."

"That's every hard, beautiful inch!"

The thought of her sucking his entire cock made his stomach muscles tightened. "Then do it!"

She pressed her face in his pubic hair, breathing deeply, as if the scent of him excited her.

Then she moved her lips over his shaft, raining hungry kisses against his pulsing length. Her moist tongue slid along the contours of his balls, heightening his passions.

"Holy hell, Sharde, that feels so good."

She gently moved her teeth along his balls before pressing heated kisses against them. She lifted her head and smiled up at him, a look of wanton desire in her dark gaze. "The taste and smell of your big balls and your hard cock makes my pussy so wet. Oh, Jeff, I am so hot...so hungry to feel your cock inside my pussy...taste it in my mouth. I want to suck your cock until you come in my mouth. I want to feel your big dick in all my openings."

He shuddered and groaned, loving the raw sensuality in her words. Damn, but she knew how to keep a man hot and hard. Feelings of lust and pleasure buffeted his body as she suddenly cupped his balls and took the head of his cock between her warm, welcoming lips.

He gritted his teeth and closed his eyes, his body trembling. He strained to hold onto his control. This was too good not to prolong.

"Hmmm." She gripped his hips and took another few inches of his eager cock into the wet warmth of her mouth.

A wave of pleasure washed over him. "Holy hell, Sharde! Stop or I'm going to come!" he warned.

She responded by sliding her hands around his body to cup his ass. She slid her lips lower along his shaft. With half his length cradled between her lips, she sucked and licked him.

It took all his willpower not to grab the back of her head and ram the rest of his aching cock into her mouth and down her throat. It had been so long since a woman had sucked him with such obvious enjoyment.

Moaning around his length, she removed one hand from his ass to cup it over his balls. Tugging gently at his hip, she pressed forward, sucking the remaining inches of his cock into the hot inferno of her mouth.

With his entire shaft surrounded by a sucking, eager mouth and his balls being gently but relentlessly squeezed, his control snapped.

"Oh, God, Sharde!" He shuddered, curled his fingers in her hair, fucked his length down her throat, and ground his groin against her face.

Moaning softly, he fucked her sweet, warm mouth, loving the feel of his cock sliding along her tongue and down her throat. She removed her hand from his balls, curled it on his ass, and eagerly accepted the hard, out of control lunges of his cock.

Damn, there was no feeling in the world like the mouth of a woman who knew how to suck cock. A wall of desire crashed over him, submerging him in a tidal wave of unmitigated lust. His climax ignited.

He tried to pull out of her as he felt his cum rushing to blast free, but she tightened her grip on his buns, sliding one finger between his cheeks.

Keeping his cock deep in her throat, she pressed a finger against his ass. Powerless to stop one the most incredible orgasms of his life, he gripped his hands over her head. Thrusting roughly into her mouth, he shot jet after jet of cum down her throat.

She swallowed eagerly, grinding her mouth against his groin. Releasing his hips, she cupped his balls, squeezing his nuts until she had milked every drop of seed from him.

Only then did she remove her lips from his cock. She pressed a kiss against his cock and balls. Still kneeling, she smiled at up at him, slowly licking her lips.

His legs shook and he dropped to his knees beside her. The unselfish manner in which she'd just coaxed him into one of the most exquisite climaxes of his life blew him away. But his response to her was not entirely physical. He felt an emotional bond with her he had not expected and wasn't sure he wanted.

In addition to an overwhelming desire to fuck her until she screamed in bliss, he wanted to take her into his arms and hold her. . .stroke her. . .kiss her. . .and tell her how special what they'd just shared was to him.

CHAPTER THREE

Her nipples hard and her panty bottoms soaked, Sharde knelt in front of Jefferson, drinking in the expression of surprised bliss on his handsome face. After years of being invisible to him as a woman, he finally knew she was a woman capable of fully satisfying his sexual needs. Now she'd need to work on satisfying his emotional ones.

She touched her trembling hand to his cheek. He turned his head and kissed her palm. "Oh, damn, Sharde!"

His voice, low and husky and filled with awe, danced along her spine like a caress.

She stroked a hand over his chest. "Did you enjoy having me suck your cock?"

"What do you think?" He pulled her close to him and drew her down to the floor to lie on her side, her body pressed against his. "Where the hell have you been all my life?"

She smiled and nibbled at his shoulder. "I'm glad you enjoyed it, Jefferson."

"Enjoyed?" He stroked a hand under her sweatshirt and along her back. She shivered in response. "Enjoy is too tame a word for what just happened. I...I...where did you learn how to tease and torture a man like that?"

She lifted her head from his shoulder and smiled up at him. "Wouldn't you like to know?"

He paused with his big hand at the top of her sweat bottoms. "Yes, I would. I thought I knew you fairly well but honey, you have hidden depths I'd love to explore."

So close to her fantasy of having him fuck her, she decided to give herself the exquisite torture of waiting a while longer. When he finally slid his big, hot cock into her aching pussy for the first time, it would be a moment she would forever treasure. If she made him wait for the pleasure, he would want her all the more and their first fuck would blow them both away.

Her older sister, Cathi, insisted pussy too freely and easily obtained was never as enjoyable for a man as pussy withheld—if even only for a few hours.

She pulled out of his embrace and rose. "Let's explore them tomorrow. Right now I'm starving and this time I want some meat I can actually eat."

He pulled his briefs on and rose. "Oh, I think you did a pretty good job of eating my meat," he told her, arching a brow. "Where did you learn to suck cock like that?"

She couldn't stop the blood from rushing to her cheeks. She averted her gaze. "I'll go and finish cooking." She sat on the floor and quickly put her socks on before moving towards the kitchen.

He reached out a hand to stop her. She reluctantly turned to face him, uncertain what she would see in his gaze. Would he think less of her now she'd allowed him to see how horny she was for him?

"Food can wait. You don't think I'm going to get my jollies and leave you without yours, do you?"

She cast a quick glance at his briefs. He was not aroused now. But that was okay. She didn't have the energy or nerve to get him hot again. Besides, she wanted him to know she had no problem pleasing him sexually without asking or expecting anything in return—yet.

"Let's eat first. We have the entire night ahead of us."

He shook his head, drawing her back into his arms. "It's not my style to leave my partner unfulfilled."

She placed her hands against his shoulders and gazed up into his eyes. "I want to enjoy the anticipation of what will happen when we go to bed, Jefferson. As I chew each piece of meat, I want to contemplate how wonderful I'll feel lying under you, full of the most delicious piece of meat I've ever had the pleasure to taste."

"Oh, shit, Sharde! You're making me horny all over again." He tightened his arms around her. She felt his cock stirring against her.

Smiling, she kissed his chest and pulled out of his arms. "Steak, anyone?"

He smacked her ass. "I'd rather have some pussy!"

And she'd rather give him some. She moistened her lips. "Steak now, pussy later."

He sighed. "Okay. Have it your way. Steak now and pussy... lots of it...later."

The muscles in her stomach tightened painfully. "Yes," she whispered, blushing again. "Lots of it."

He reached for his socks and jeans.

With one last look at his body she headed to the kitchen. Ten minutes later, she felt a draft.

She turned to see him at the cabin door. "Where are you going?"

"I'm going out to the shed to bring in enough wood for the rest of the night and tomorrow morning. I'm thinking we're not going to want to stir once we start fucking."

Thoughts of a night spent in his arms made her hot all over. The heat in her face seemed to spread to her entire body.

He studied her face. "Does my use of the word fucking offend you? Is it too crude?"

"No," she admitted. "I…love the thought that you want to fuck me."

"Then why are you blushing?"

"Just because I love it doesn't mean I'm used to it."

"So you're used to men who dress it up?"

"Yes, but I prefer it raw and real with you, Jeff."

"Raw and real coming up, honey."

She nodded, her heart thumping in her chest.

Smiling, he left the cabin.

Half an hour later, they sat across from each other at the small table in the kitchen pushing their steak and potatoes around on their plates. She had a glass of red wine while he had a beer.

"How do you want to handle this?" he asked.

"Handle what?"

He set his beer can down and reached across the table to hold her hand. "Our sleeping together will complicate our working together."

So he'd abandoned raw and real already? Not a good sign. She swallowed hard. He also sounded as if he regretted allowing her to suck him earlier. "What do you mean?"

He sighed. "Actually, I've been thinking our having sex would be a bad thing, Sharde."

She fought back panic. Just when she was soaring, thinking they were halfway to an intimate relationship, he snatched her back down to earth. She tightened her lips. Hell would freeze over before she allowed him to get out of fucking her senseless at least once that weekend.

She made an effort to keep her voice steady as she spoke. "There's nothing to handle. We can enjoy each other while we're here. When we leave…we leave just as we arrived…as colleagues and friends."

"And you could deal with that?"

Like she had a choice? She pushed her plate away and walked around the small table to stand in front of him. When he looked up, she stroked her fingers through his dark hair. "You're nuts if you think I'm not getting at least one hot, raunchy fuck out of you, Jeff!" She unzipped his jeans, slid her hand inside the slit in his briefs and curled her fingers over his warm flesh. "I want this cock in my pussy and damn you, I'm going to have it there!"

He gently removed her hand from his jeans. "Don't misunderstand me. I want you too..."

"But?"

He brought the hand he still held up to his mouth. He pressed a kiss in her palm. "But we need to be realistic, honey."

"The only reality we're going to deal with this weekend, Jeff, is that I need some cock and I'm getting some of yours. Is that clear?"

"Crystal."

"Then what's your problem?"

"Can you deal with a casual, but sexual relationship between us, Sharde? Because that's all I have to give now. And I swear you are the last woman in the world I'd ever want to hurt or disappoint."

She wanted so much more, but that was enough to begin with. She sat on his lap, linking her arms around his neck. "They really hurt you, didn't they?"

The muscles in his jaw clenched and he made no effort to hold her. "I don't want to talk about them, Sharde." His gaze flicked over her face. "And I don't want to risk hurting you..."

Like I've been hurt. The unspoken words hung in the air between them. She lifted his hands and placed them under sweatshirt on her breasts. "What makes you think there's any danger of that?"

He cupped his hands over her breasts, squeezing gently. "I don't know there is…I just don't want to ruin our relationship. I depend on you. I'd rather have you as a friend and colleague than a lover."

So she had overrated how well she had managed to satisfy him. She rose and walked back to her seat, her face hot, and an ache in her chest that made breathing difficult. "I see."

"Isn't that what you'd rather? Lovers come and go with alarming frequency, Sharde, but friendship hopefully lasts forever."

She picked up her glass and sipped her wine. "Who says we can't be both? At least for this weekend? When we get out of here, we can look on this as just…a sweet interlude. Or didn't you enjoy being intimate with me?"

"Of course, I did. You know I did. But I'm afraid of hurting you."

"Don't be. I'm an adult. I appreciate your concern, but I can take care of myself. Right now I just need…a little…some hot, uncomplicated, uncommitted sex. Why is that so wrong, Jefferson?"

He reached across the table and clasped her hand in his. "It's not. If you can promise me you won't end up hurt and we can go back to what we had when we leave here, I'll spend the weekend fucking you until you can barely walk."

She took several gulps of her wine and sat down her glass. "Why don't we sleep on it and think about it in the morning?" She eased her hand from his. Picking up her plate and glass, she rose.

He picked up his plate and followed her to the sink. He set his plate on the counter and leaned against her back, pressing his cheek against hers. "Sharde…I want you, but I don't want to hurt you." He brushed his lips against her cheek. "You are too important to me."

She took a deep breath before turning to face him. "You're making too much of this, Jefferson. Let's just live for the moment...this weekend." She slipped her arms around his neck, stroking her fingers through the hair at the nape of his neck. "I really need a fuck. Do me?"

She looked up at him and saw desire in the gray eyes staring down at her. His nostrils flared. He touched her hair and cheeks. "You have such beautiful hair and such a lovely skin tone...such sweet lips. I had no idea you were such a sweet, sexy, passionate woman." His mouth touched hers in a fleeting movement that was more a request for permission to continue than it was a kiss.

She leaned into him, parting her lips under his. "Just for this weekend...be mine? Be my man and let me be your woman. I'll make you a very happy man."

His arms tightened around her. "There's no doubt about that," he murmured. He kissed her. It wasn't really a kiss, he devoured her, his lips burning and searing the masculine taste of his mouth into hers. She felt as if he was branding her with his kiss, and she loved it.

His big hands slid under her sweatshirt to caress her back. He pressed her closer, forcing her breasts against his chest. She surrendered to the pressure of his mouth on hers, allowing her head to loll against his shoulder. His tongue touched hers and the embers of desire coiled in her belly ignited.

She raked her fingers through his hair, moaning softly as the fire of her love and desire for him burned inside her, incinerating every thought and consideration except the need to get as close to him as possible.

She felt him hardening against her. This time he was going

to be inside her. She slid her hands up his body, pushing up his sweater. Feeling as if she would melt if she didn't feel him inside her, she broke their heated kiss to pull out of his arms. Breathing deeply, she yanked his shirt and tee shirt from his jeans. She ran her hands over his tight, washboard abs, down to the top of his jeans.

She fumbled with the button holding his jeans closed. Her hands shook and she couldn't manage it. "Help me!"

He brushed her hands away. Stepping away from her, he quickly undressed.

Her heart hammered in her chest as he stood before her, naked and aroused. He had a big, beautiful, muscular body with wide shoulders, hard abs, long legs, and lean hips. His long, thick weeping cock, beckoned to her.

She looked at him, licking her lips, a rush of lust and desire filling her pussy. "Oh, Jefferson! I need you!"

"You can have me, honey." He moved closer, threading his fingers into her hair. He kissed her slowly, rubbing his cock against her. She whimpered against his lips, so hot for him she could almost taste her desire. "Jefferson...please."

He sucked her bottom lip, sliding a hand down her back. He moved his hand into her sweat bottoms to cup a palm over her butt. The feel of his hand on the bare skin of her ass sent a series of chills through her.

She gasped and reached between their bodies to hold his cock. He felt thick, hot, hard, and utterly delicious against her fingers.

He dragged his mouth from hers and stepped back. She reluctantly released his cock and opened her eyes. Then the breath caught in her throat. Tiny fires of desire burned in his silver-gray gaze.

She had dreamed of seeing that look for so long. Now that

she did, it was hard to reconcile that this was actually happening. Or was it yet another dream from which she would wake to find herself alone?

He moved closer and reached for the bottom of her sweatshirt. He kissed her and pulled it over her head, revealing the black lace bra of the teddy, which barely covered her large breasts.

He took but a moment to study her upper body before he dropped to his knees, reaching for her right foot. She lifted it and he pulled off first one sock and then the other. Rising, he kissed her slowly, deeply.

Still not certain this wasn't a dream, she parted her lips, savoring the raw hunger she tasted in his kiss. His hands slid down her body to the waistband of her sweatpants. Keeping contact with her mouth, he pushed the sweats over her hips. His fingers brushing over her bare thighs seemed to burn her skin. He pulled his mouth away from hers and stepped back to remove her pants.

She swallowed slowly, standing before him in the skimpy black teddy she had bought with hopes of this moment with him in mind. The top of the teddy lifted, separated, and showcased her breasts, particularly her nipples, which peeked out at him from twin lace holes. The high cut of the bottom of the teddy exposed her inner thighs and butt.

Taking a deep breath, she parted her legs, revealing the strategically cut hole in the teddy.

She saw his Adam's apple working. "Holy hell, Sharde! God, you're dark and lovely...so...lovely."

He sounded surprised.

She lifted her chin, allowing a small, wanton smile to touch her lips. Her face might not turn many heads, but she knew her body would. His gaze danced over her breasts, over her stomach, down her legs and back up her body to center on her groin.

"And for this weekend, I'm all yours, Jefferson."

He made a small sound and took her hand in his. He led her over to the fire and drew her down to the sleeping bag. She lay on her back with her legs parted, still afraid this was a sweet dream.

He moved close to her, lying on his side with his cock, hard and hot, poking her leg. Almost afraid to breathe, she turned her head. She felt his breath on her face. He was too close for her to see the expression in his eyes.

He touched his tongue to her throat. A jolt of electricity danced through her.

"You like that?" he demanded softly.

"Yes…oh, yes."

He cupped one hand under her neck, allowing the other one to brush against her nipples until they were hard, aching peaks. Satisfied, he stroked his free hand down her body, over her stomach, to cup her in his palm.

He rubbed her gently. She closed her eyes, sinking her teeth into her bottom lip. This felt so good it had to be a dream. He moved his head, finding her mouth with his. As he kissed her, he reached between her legs to part her wet, aching folds. He slipped a finger into her pussy.

His lips over hers smothered the small whimpers of pleasure forced from her lips as he added a second finger inside her. She shuddered, closing her legs over his probing fingers, the muscles in her stomach so tight they almost ached.

She opened her eyes and looked at him. "Please, Jefferson! Please! Fuck me now!"

His eyes burned with a level of desire that made her feel weak. "Oh, I plan to please you, but I'm going to have to use my fingers and my mouth. I don't have a condom," he groaned against her lips.

She was too close to having her ultimate fantasy fulfilled and too far gone to be able to think rationally. "I'm on the pill and I haven't been with a man without a condom in nearly ten years," she whispered, not knowing or caring what she said. She wanted him so badly she was prepared to do and say anything to have him inside her.

"I haven't been with a woman without one in several years, but are you sure?"

"Yes!"

"Sharde, I'm so hungry, once I get inside you, I'm not going to be able to pull out until after I come. You need to be sure you want to do this without a condom."

"I'm very sure. I'm on the pill and we're both safe."

Still he hesitated.

She touched his cheek, feeling desperation threatening to overwhelm her. "Jeff! Fuck me now or else!"

"Or else what?"

"Or else I'll make you one sorry bastard!"

Smiling, he eased her onto her back. Rising over her, he balanced most of his weight on his extended arms. She eagerly parted her legs, wet and ready for him. He settled between her thighs.

She looked down their bodies. Her lips parted and her heart hammered wildly. His large, heavy length with the big, almost purple head rested against the riot of dark hair surrounding the entrance to her pussy. The contrast of their skin colors increased her level of excitement.

Please, God. Don't let this dream end before he slides his cock into me.

He lay above her, looking down their bodies. He lifted his

head and looked down at her. "I can smell your pussy...fragrant and musky...I love the smell."

"You're going to love the feel too, if you ever decide to come inside!"

He laughed. "Somebody needs some cock big time."

"Somebody is going to get some big cock—now!" She placed her hands over his hips, gave a jerk, and pushed her butt off the sleeping bag.

The big, hard head of his cock slid between her wet folds and into her body. Although she would have welcomed it, he didn't plunge in and take complete and immediate possession of her. He entered her slowly, clearly savoring the coming together of their heated flesh.

She closed her eyes, awash in incredible sensations as he pushed into her, stretching and filling her with a wonderful fullness that made her toes curls and her back arch.

"Oh, lord you feel so good going in," she moaned. Eager to take all of him inside her, she kept her hips off the sleeping bag until she felt his pubic hair come to rest against hers. "Oooh..."

Fully seated inside her hot pussy, he pushed his hips down, driving her back to the sleeping bag. He settled on top of her, one hand still cupping her neck, the other slipping under her body to palm her butt.

She gasped and he found her mouth, stroking his tongue inside as he began to move in and out of her with an exquisite slowness that sent tremors of bliss all through her. The delicious heat and tension where his body stroked and pushed into hers overwhelmed her senses and made her fall ever deeper in love with him.

He made sweet, breathtaking love to her. She contracted her stuffed pussy around his cock, urging him to take her with a fierceness that would bind them together in a blaze of gratifying lust and love. But he took his time, his deep, leisurely thrusts and his feverish kisses gradually branding her as his as a sweet heat slowly invaded her body. The tension and pleasure built in her until her climax thundered through her, leaving her sobbing and clinging to him.

Resting his full weight on her, he held her. He whispered in her ear that she was sweet and wonderful as wave after wave of satisfaction washed over her. She eagerly allowed herself to be submerged under a wall of absolute bliss.

When her senses returned, he lay on top of her, his lips against her forehead, his extended arms bearing most of his weight. She immediately realized with a delicious delight, that he was still erect and still inside her.

"Oh, Jeff!" Feeling lethargic, but determined to please him again, she locked her legs over the back of his thighs and drew his head down to hers. As their lips touched, she shuddered and tightened herself around him, grinding her hips against him.

Lord, she loved the feel of his cock inside her, hard and hot as he increased the tempo of their fuck. He groaned against her mouth, thrusting his length deep and hard into her. He kept thrusting hard until he stiffened. "Oh, holy hell, Sharde!" Sliding his hands down to her hips, he held them still and pummeled her body with powerful, lustful strokes that sent a new wave of heat and desire through her.

Lord, she felt as if she were losing her mind. She held him tight, thrusting back at him. Finally, he groaned, called out her name again, and roughly pushed and pulled his cock in and out of her until jet after jet of cum shot from his cock into her receptive pussy.

"Hell!" He collapsed on top of her, buried his face against her neck, small aftershocks shaking his body. She held him, stroking her hands over his damp back. After several long, sweet moments, he pulled out of her, rolled on to his back, and drew her onto his body.

He pulled the cover spread over the sleeping bag up and pressed a soft, sweet kiss against her lips. "Holy hell, honey, that was..."

"Good?"

He tightened his arms around her waist. "No. It was incredible...just incredible...you're incredible."

She smiled down at him, loving the way the firelight played over his handsome face. "You think you might want some more pussy before we leave?"

He curled his fingers in her hair and lifted her head from his shoulder, a frown on his face. "I don't want you to think this is just about sex, Sharde. You know I care about you...don't you?"

She'd never doubted his concern for her. What she craved was his desire and love. "Yes."

"I don't want you to think I just want pussy from you."

"I know, Jeff. But just for this weekend, there's nothing wrong with your wanting pussy and my lusting for your big cock...is there?"

"No."

"Then you'll be wanting some more pussy?"

"Now that I've had a taste of it, you're going to be hard-pressed to keep my cock out of your pussy."

"You can have as much pussy as you can handle, handsome."

"Really? How about another fuck now, then?"

He released her hair and she reached between their bodies to feed his cock into her body. When he was balls deep inside her, she curled her fingers in his hair and they enjoyed a quick, scorching fuck.

They came within moments of each other. Feeling happy and sated, she pressed her face against his shoulder. The first step in her plan to capture him was complete. They had both been satisfied. Now all she had to do was get him to need a steady diet of sex with her. Then she'd work on making him fall as deeply in love with her as she was with him. How difficult could that be, now that she was fairly certain she had him hooked on sex with her?

CHAPTER FOUR

Jefferson woke in the middle of the night, wanting Sharde again. The only light in the living room came from the fire. He lay on his side, watching the firelight play over her face. As she rested on her back, her long, dark hair was spread out across her face. She looked content and surprisingly pretty.

He slipped out of the sleeping bag and rose. Without the warmth of her body and the covers, there was a distinct chill against his naked body. He removed the guard from the fire-place, added more wood, banked it, replaced the guard, and slipped back into the sleeping bag with her.

"Jeff?" She turned into his arms, pressing close and seeking his mouth. Their lips touched and he slid on top of her, reaching down to stroke his fingers between her legs and into her body.

He stroked and kissed her until the moisture against his fingers signaled her readiness for sex. Then he sucked her neck as he thrust his cock into her hot, delicious pussy. Sinking deep into her slick heat felt like coming home. He felt a tender lust for her he hadn't experienced with any of his other lovers.

She moaned, stroking her fingers along his back.

"Oh, damn, honey, you are so hot...and so sweet...so tight...you enchant me..."

She stroked her fingers through his hair. "Love me," she whispered.

"Oh, yes, honey." He thrust hard into her.

She gasped and pushed her hands against his shoulders. "No. I don't want a fuck...this time I want you to make love to me...as if you care about me."

"I do care about you. I always have and I always will."

"Prove it to me. Love me."

He made love to her slowly, savoring and fully enjoying the experience. Everything about her excited him, from the taste of her lips, the feel of her large, lovely breasts crushed under his chest, the way her pussy caressed and held his cock as if the two were made for each other, to her smooth, dark skin which reminded him of black silk.

He couldn't ever remember any other woman engaging all his senses as she did. This definitely was not just sex. Each time he pulled his cock almost all the way out of her before slowly sinking it back into her tight, hot pussy, a soft, blissful moan escaped her full lips and his heart hammered. For the first time in years, he was more interested in ensuring his partner's pleasure before seeking his own. If this is what great sex with a woman who was also his friend was about, he'd been a fool not to try it before.

The smell of sex filled his nostrils and a hunger to taste her tightened his gut. Gripping her hips, he pulled his cock out of her, pushed the covers away, and quickly slid down her body.

Sprawling between her legs, he parted the wet folds of her vagina, revealing her fragrant pink pussy. "Damn, you have a pretty pussy, honey."

"It was made just for your pleasure," she told him in a wanton voice. "Do whatever you want to and with it."

He stroked two fingers inside her, loving the way her inner muscles creamed them. Eager to taste her, he extended his tongue to taste her moist flesh.

She shuddered. "Oh, lord, Jeff…eat me."

"Oh, yeah, honey." Pressing his face closer, he stroked his fingers inside her while nibbling at her outer lips and raking his tongue against her clit.

He ate her hungrily, greedily, his senses awash in the musky aroma of her, delighting in the way her body shook and the half-sobs filling the room as he did. The taste, smell, and texture of her pussy drove him wild. Flicking his tongue against her clit, he thrust his fingers inside her until she screamed his name, her body shuddering.

Withdrawing his fingers, he gripped her flailing hips, closed his mouth over her climaxing pussy and licked and slurped at her as she came against his mouth and tongue.

When he was sure he'd lapped up most of her moisture, he slid up her body, thrust his cock back into her pussy, and cupped her face between his palms.

"Open your eyes and look at me."

Her eyes fluttered opened and a sense of masculine pride filled him as he noted the look of bliss in her gaze. "Now taste yourself on my lips and tongue," he whispered.

Smiling, she drew him down to her. Sliding her hands on his ass, she parted her lips and welcomed his tongue into her mouth. Feeling as if he was where he belonged, and forgetting her wish to be made love to, he fucked her roughly until he exploded inside her.

He loved the way she held him tight, keeping her groin against his, as if she were eager to ensure every drop of his cum remained inside her.

Still buried in her pussy, he collapsed in her arms. After a moment, he rolled onto his back so her body sprawled on top of his. "Damn, you keep this up and you'll ruin me for any other woman."

She murmured something, pressing her cheek against his shoulder.

He threaded his fingers through her hair. "What?"

"I said that's the plan."

He closed his fingers in her hair. "What plan?"

"What are you muttering about?" she asked, her voice low and almost inaudible. "Go to sleep before I decide I want you again."

Releasing her hair, he drifted to sleep.

In the morning he woke alone in the sleeping bag. He turned his head. She stood in the kitchen wearing his shirt and his socks, leaving her long, big legs bare. He stretched and slipped out of the sleeping bag, the smell of coffee tickling his nose.

She turned and looked at him. "'Morning."

With her dark hair hanging in a wild cloud around her face, she looked both sweet and sexy. How had he ever thought her anything but pretty? He smiled. "Good morning." Ignoring the urge to sweep her into his arms and kiss her senseless, he made his way to the bathroom. He brushed his teeth and did a quick wash in the cold room before heading back to the kitchen with a towel wrapped around his waist.

She stood in the kitchen with her back to him, sipping coffee. As he approached she put her coffee cup down, turned, smiled, opened his shirt, and flashed him. "See anything you like?"

She had removed the sexy teddy from the night before. He got his first view of her naked body. She had large, firm breasts, a flat stomach, and long, shapely legs. She was big without being fat. His gaze dropped to the dark triangular patch of curls between her legs and his cock hardened.

He tossed the towel aside and crossed the room to her. Catching her around her waist, he turned her, eased her against the wall, and parted her legs.

She pressed against his shoulders. "Breakfast will get cold."

"The only breakfast I'm interested in now is your pussy."

She smiled. "You sound like a man on his way to being addicted to it."

"Not on the way...already there," he whispered. Nibbling at her neck, he stroked his fingers into her.

Soon she was moist and ready for him. He thrust into her. She felt so good and tight, he slid balls deep with one greedy movement.

He linked his fingers through hers, licked her neck, and gave her a fast, furious fuck. She thrust her soft, rounded butt back at him. He loved the feel of her body against his. Sliding one hand down her body, he found her clit.

"Oooh. Oh, yes!" she whispered, her feminine muscles tightening around him.

He shuddered and increased and deepened his thrusts, rubbing his thumb over her clit each time he pulled halfway out of her. The wild tremors inside her set him off and they exploded in quick succession.

He pulled out of her and kissed her. "Damn, but you are so sweet."

She laughed against his lips, slapped his ass, and pushed him away. "It's about time you noticed."

"What's that supposed to mean?"

She shrugged. "I've been under your nose for nine years, Jeff!"

"Nine years? Are you saying—"

"I'm not saying anything except that I'm feeling adventurous this morning."

Hungry to experience every conceivable form of sex with her, he caught her around her waist and pressed her, breasts forward, against the wall. He raked his teeth against the side of her neck. "How adventurous are you feeling?"

"What do you have in mind?"

The note of barely suppressed excitement in her voice boded well for the rest of the weekend. He slid one hand around her body to cup her pussy. "You have a lovely ass."

She stiffened against him. "My...you want to...up my ass..."

She couldn't seem to finish the sentence and he decided she wasn't into anal sex. Since he had no protection, it was a moot point. He kissed her neck and stroked his hands over her big, warm ass. "Would you let me...if I'd come prepared with a condom?"

"I don't just allow any Tom, Dick, or Jefferson to poke around up my ass."

He moved away from her.

She turned to face him.

They considered each other in silence before she spoke again. "If you want anal sex, you're going to need more than a weekend pass, Jeff."

He sighed, visions of sliding his cock between her lovely dark cheeks and into her puckered anus teasing him. "I see."

"Good." She buttoned his shirt and ran her tongue along her lips. "Coffee?"

What he really wanted was to thrust his cock up her sweet looking ass, but he raked his hands through his hair, nodding. As she poured his coffee, he went back to the bathroom for another quick, cold wash. In the bedroom, he dressed quickly, his thoughts on Sharde and the unexpected turn their relationship had taken.

She was the last woman he had expected to find attractive. Yet sex with her went beyond just sex. When he was inside her, he felt a sense of belonging. During and after sex, it felt almost as if there was a more important and elemental connection between them. Something soft, warm, and nurturing in her reached out to touch and heal the hurt in him.

He supposed that's why he found it almost impossible to keep his hands off her over the next few days. Each night he went to sleep with her in his arms. Each morning he woke eager to see her and to make love to her again.

When they ventured out for a walk Sunday, he held her hand, even when there was no danger of her slipping or falling. She was soft and warm, exciting and wonderful.

Ben often told him that if he expected to be happy in a relationship with a woman, he was going to have to start to ignore the trees and search for the forest, meaning he thought Jefferson placed too much emphasis on a woman's looks.

Considering how badly his last two relationships had ended, he supposed Ben was right. Not that Ben would approve of his sleeping with Sharde. Ben was a big believer that business and pleasure should not be mixed.

He grinned. Oh well. Ben could sleep with whoever he wanted to and allow him to do the same.

The weekend seemed to fly past and his lovemaking on Sunday night held a tinge of desperation. He woke several times during the night to hold and kiss her. On Monday morning, they woke early, had sex, ate a quick breakfast, had sex again, and then packed up to head home.

As they left the cabin, he felt as if he were leaving an important part of himself. He could detect no reluctance on her part to leaving. Yet she'd hinted at having feelings for him that went beyond the purely physical...feelings she'd also implied she'd held for a while. Or had he, carried away by lust, read more into what she'd said than she'd intended?

They didn't talk much on the drive back to Philly. He kept his gaze on the road and his thoughts on her. They had agreed that when they returned home their relationship would return to normal. The road ahead was clear. He cast a quick look at her. She had her head turned away from him, staring out the passenger window.

It was warm inside the cab of the SUV and she had removed her coat. Her neck was bare and he felt a sudden urge to lean over and lick the side of her neck. He gave himself a mental shake and turned his attention back to the road.

They had another two-hour drive before they got home—unless he could find a way to lengthen their time together. "Do you want to stop for dinner?"

"Sounds temping, but I'm tired. I'm looking forward to a long hot soak and an early night."

Was he the only one dreading their arrival home and the end it would mean for their physical relationship? "How about a coffee pit stop?"

She yawned. "I'd rather not, Jefferson."

She sounded eager to get away from him. And he'd been vain enough to fear her wanting to extend their relationship once they returned to the office.

"Why not?"

"I'm tired. It's not like I got much sleep this weekend," she pointed out.

"Are you complaining?"

"No. Just explaining why I'm tired and want to go straight home without any unnecessary stops."

They made the rest of the drive in silence. At her condo, he got out and went around to open her door. She ignored the hand he extended and slipped out, making sure not to touch him.

He got her suitcase from the back. She reached for it. He shook his head. "I'll carry it inside."

"That's not necessary, Jefferson."

"I know, but I just want to do it."

She shrugged. "Thanks."

He used his remote to lock the SUV's door and arm the alarm before he followed her inside. Her condo was on the third floor. He followed her inside, setting her suitcase just inside the door.

She hesitated before turning to look at him.

"Are you sorry?" He hadn't meant to ask the question and was annoyed with himself.

She smiled and shook her head. "No. Are you?"

He looked at her; her hair was in its usual, unassuming bun. What had happened to the uninhibited woman who had given him one of the most incredible weekends of his life? "No." He felt awkward because he wanted to kiss her but knew that was out of the question.

She took off her jacket and held it over one arm. "I'd offer you coffee, but all I have is instant and I'm really tired."

And apparently eager to see him go. He nodded. "Okay. I'll see you in the office in the morning."

She nodded. "I'll be there."

He stuffed his hands into his jacket pockets and looked at her. He really wanted a last kiss. There was nothing in her cool gaze to indicate she would welcome that. He sighed and headed for the door.

She followed and he turned to look down at her. She met his gaze briefly before looking away. He bent his head.

She placed a hand against his shoulder, shaking her head. "Good night, Jefferson."

"What will one last kiss hurt?" He didn't wait for her reply, but leaned down and pressed his lips against the corner of her mouth. She made a soft sound and turned to face him, slipping her arms around his neck.

He licked her lips, holding her close. "Can I spend the night?"

She shuddered against him. "No."

"Okay. How about a few hours? I promise I won't stay long. I just want one last…kiss."

"You just had one." She drew her mouth away from his. "We agreed once we were home we'd go back to normal, Jefferson. We're home and we don't normally sleep together."

He swallowed, thoughts of one last night with her filling him with a feverish longing. "We could do normal tomorrow when we get to work."

"Or we could stick to our agreement and do it now." She pushed against his shoulders.

"Sharde—"

"Jeff! Please."

Sighing, he released her.

She walked to the door and held it open. "The weekend's over."

"Didn't you enjoy it?"

"You know I did, but we had an agreement and we need to stick to it."

"Why?"

"Because that's the only way this will work."

He shook his head. "We've been very close for eight of the nine years we've known each other. We can make anything we want work."

"Right now you're thinking with your cock and that always gets you in trouble, Jeff."

"What the hell is that suppose to mean?"

She closed her eyes briefly. "I'm sorry. That comment was way out of line."

"Damn right it was."

"We're both tired and saying and thinking things we shouldn't. Let's say good night while we're still friends."

"Friendship is overrated." Annoyed that he'd be going to bed with blue balls, he turned to leave.

She touched his arm. "Jeff, please...don't leave angry...not after we shared such a great weekend."

"I'm more horny and frustrated than I am angry."

"You set the rules." She squeezed his arm. "Good night."

"Good night, honey."

He left and she closed the door. He stood waiting until he heard her locks sliding into place. Feeling as if he'd been kicked to the curb, he left the building. He drove home, had a couple of hot dogs and several beers, took a shower, and went to bed. He lay awake for a long time thinking of Sharde before he finally drifted to sleep.

***

The next morning, after a restless night, Sharde sat in her office going over résumés for systems analysts with Darbi. Darbi had chosen twenty out of the hundred e-resumes for Sharde to give closer consideration.

She was tired and had trouble focusing. "Who did you say I should take closer looks at again?"

Darbi sat back in her chair. "You don't seem very rested or very happy. How did the weekend go...or shouldn't I ask?"

Sharde sighed and sipped her coffee. She could hardly admit that she and Jefferson had spent the majority of the weekend having sex. Nor could she confess that she had spent most of the previous night wishing she'd allowed Jefferson to stay with her.

She frowned. If she couldn't tell Darbi, who could she tell? She shrugged. "There was no power and that made for chilly nights." Not that she'd felt much chill wrapped in Jefferson's arms. "Or it would have…if we hadn't…"

"Wasn't he worth…did he disappoint?"

"In bed?" Her cheeks burned. "No! But he's only interested in sex…nothing more."

"Are you sure you can't make that enough?"

"Yes!" She shook her head. "I thought it might be enough… but making love with him just made me want his love."

"And you don't think that's possible?"

She sighed. "I don't know…I just don't know. I'll see what the coming weeks bring. But right now I feel as if I just need a mini vacation to recover from my mini vacation."

"Do you regret spending the weekend with him?"

"No. I might find later that I do, but right now…no."

"Then why are you sure sex won't be enough?"

"Because I love him and while the sex was great…I need more than that."

Darbi sighed. "I think when I'm ready for another relationship, I'm not going to look for or expect love."

"I know you've been hurt, but surely you're not giving up on love."

"Love hurts and I have no desire to be hurt again. The next time I will be content with a man who's interested enough to wait for marriage before the sex, who treats me well and excites me physically."

Sharde blinked. "Where are you going to find a man willing to wait for marriage before he insists on sex?"

Darbi shrugged, a smile tugging at her lips. "I have no idea. Maybe that's why I'm feeling lonely and soooo horny."

Their gazes met and locked and they burst into peals of helpless laugher.

A knock on Sharde's office door finally silenced their laughter. She wiped tears from her eyes and took a deep, calming breath. "Come in," she called.

The door opened and Jefferson walked in. He paused when he saw Darbi. "Am I interrupting?"

"Ah...well actually Darbi and I are deciding on analysts to ask to come in for interviews. Was there something you needed from either one of us?"

"Actually, I was hoping for a word with you, Sharde."

Darbi gathered her folders and cup and rose. She looked at Sharde. "I need to check on my plans for the trip to L.A. Call me when you're ready to go over these again."

She nodded. "Thanks, Darbi."

Darbi nodded at Jefferson. He nodded back, holding the door open for her. He closed it after her, leaning back against it.

During the night Sharde had decided that the next phase in Operation Seduce Jefferson would be playing hard to get. He'd had a taste of her passion and now she was going to make him want more so badly he'd realize she had more to offer than just sex. She forced herself to meet his gaze. "What's up?"

"How are you?"

"I'm fine. How are you?"

He raked a hand through his hair. "I'm tired. I didn't sleep well last night as you might imagine. What about you?"

She shrugged, looked him in the eye, and lied. "I had a bath, a sandwich, a glass of wine, and slept all night."

"Did you?"

"Yes."

"I wish I could say the same."

She looked down at the printouts on her desk. "Was there something I could do for you?"

"I want to get the budget set. I thought maybe we could crunch figures over lunch."

She glanced up at him, not quite meeting his gaze. "When?"

"Today. Are you free?"

"No. I have plans."

He thrust his hands in his pant pockets. "Can you change them?"

"I'd rather not. They're longstanding."

"What about after lunch? Coffee?"

"I really need to decide who to ask in for interviews. We need to get people hired and up to speed as soon as possible if we're not going to be outbid again by Fra-Tech."

The muscles in his face tightened. "We are not going to come in second to them again!"

She wondered how much of the determination she saw in his gaze was based not only on having lost a big contract to Fra-Tech, but also on having lost Vanessa to the handsome owner, Clayton Frazier.

"Then we need to be ready."

"I know that, but the budget is important too so we'll know how much we can afford to offer in terms of salary and benefits."

"I know. Tell you what. I'll get together with Nelson in accounting and we'll crunch the numbers, and I'll get a report to you ASAP."

He shrugged. "Fine." He hesitated, his gaze sweeping over her face. "Or we could do dinner."

She deliberately misunderstood him. "Fine. I'll see if Nelson is free for dinner. If he is, we'll burn the midnight oil and have the numbers for you sometime tomorrow. How's that?"

His gaze narrowed and his lips tightened. "That's not what I had in mind, Sharde."

She went on misunderstanding him. "I don't see how we can get it done any sooner."

His gaze cooled. "Fine. Enjoy your dinner with Nelson." He turned, pulled the door opened and left, closing it softly behind him.

She sat back in her seat, a small smile tugging at her lips. He'd looked ready to blow his stack. How long would it be before he came right out and asked to see her without the pretense of it being work related? Her smile vanished. That could take weeks...unless she gave him another push.

But business came first. She checked the office phone list on her computer and reached for the phone. "Accounting. Nelson," a male voice announced in her ear.

"Hi, Nelson. This is Donovan in administration. Are you free to work late tonight with me?"

CHAPTER FIVE

"How long are you going to keep pulling his chain?"

"Pulling his chain?" Seated next to Darbi in a sauna several nights later, Sharde frowned. "What makes you think I'm pulling Jeff's chain?"

"He's asked you out three times this week and you've refused each time."

"So how is that pulling his chain?"

Darbi shrugged. "I don't know. I mean...well, he just looks so...tense and frustrated lately. And he's taken to lying in wait for me."

Sharde stiffened. "What do you mean?"

"I mean lately I'm nearly tripping over him. If I go into the coffee room, he's right behind me. When I arrive at work in the morning, he's hanging in the parking lot waiting to hold the door open for me. Today, he asked me to have lunch with him."

Sharde swallowed. "Did you?"

"No. I had plans, but he implied he'd ask me again."

"I...I didn't know he was..."

"Interested in me? He's not. He wants to pick my brain about information about you. I think maybe you need to give him a break before he explodes."

She closed her eyes briefly. "Oh, girl, you scared me. For a moment, I thought you and he..."

"Me and him? Never!" She shook her head. "No offense, Sharde, but I prefer my men a lot darker."

"None taken. I didn't set out to fall in love with him...it

just happened. When he hired me, he was struggling to get the company off the ground and we worked a lot of overtime together. More than one night, we worked so late we fell asleep in the office...me on the sofa and him in a chair. One night, while we were working, he asked if I'd mind if he put the radio on so he could listen to the World Series. Since I had set my VCR to tape it in case I missed it, I said no. That night we discovered we had a lot in common and we liked each other. At least he liked me and I fell in love with him. I don't know when it happened. One night I went to sleep really liking him a lot...the next morning I woke up in love with him.

"Until that happened, I'd planned to get a few years' experience in here and then head out to work in Atlanta. Instead, I've spent the last several years waiting for him to wake up and realize we should be more than friends."

"I think he realizes that now, Sharde."

"He realizes he wants to be my lover. I want more than that from him."

"Isn't part of getting to that point going out with him?"

"Yes...when he wants more than sex. Does that make me sound hard?"

She shook her head. "No. You have to do what you feel is right. Just don't push him too hard too fast. It can't be easy for him...after being betrayed by two women he loved in such a short time."

"It's his own fault for being so bloody stupid! I knew the moment I saw Vanessa she was a bitch! All he could see was her shaking her bony behind at him."

"Likes bony asses, huh?"

Sharde arched a brow. "Not anymore."

Darbi laughed. "I heard that, girl."

"Tomorrow's Friday. Any plans?"

"Jadan has this new male strip club she wants to check out," she said of a mutual friend. "She's heard about this hot dancer named Sarro. Do you want to come with us to ogle him?"

"Hmmm. Sounds like fun, but the only man I'm interested in ogling is Jefferson. We have a meeting tomorrow afternoon."

"You going to cut him some slack?"

"Maybe. I don't know." She sighed. "But how is Jadan? I haven't seen her in a while."

"You know Jadan."

"What is Tom going to say about her ogling some gorgeous stripper?"

"I don't think they're an item anymore."

"Oh. How's she taking that?"

"Better than I thought."

"Well, say hi for me. And while you two are ogling your gorgeous stripper, I'll be plotting Jeff's downfall."

"Sounds like a plan."

Smiling, Sharde closed her eyes, forming a mental picture of Jefferson. One of these days he was going to be hers. "Oh, yeah."

The next day, Sharde took a long lunch to go shopping for lingerie at Victoria's Secret. Recalling Jefferson's reaction to the teddy she'd worn at the cabin, she bought a skimpy red teddy with spaghetti straps. It was called a strappy-back baby-doll. Without the matching thong, it left the sides of her breasts, thighs, and ass exposed. All he'd have to do was lift up the front, part her legs, and enter her.

When she returned to the office, she took her hair down and shook it out, running her fingers through it. Looking in the mirror in her private bathroom, she decided she'd managed to achieve the look she wanted, as if a lover had been stroking his fingers through her hair.

She freshened her lipstick, unbuttoned the top two buttons of her blouse, revealing her cleavage, and waited. Right on time for their two o'clock meeting, a knock sounded on her door.

She rose, walked over to the next to lowest file cabinet in her office, bent over so that the short black skirt rose up the back of her thighs and called out, "Come in."

The door opened. She heard a quick inhalation. Still bending, she looked over her shoulder. "Be with you in a second, Jeff. Just need a few files."

He stood by the closed door staring at the backs of her thighs. Pretending not to notice, she turned back to the file cabinet, pulled two files out, and straightened. "Got them."

She sat down and motioned to the chair in front of her desk. "Have a seat."

He sat, his gaze going to her hair.

She opened the folders on her desk and glanced up at him. "We'll start interviewing for the system analysts positions on Monday." She tapped the top folder on her desk. "I have the monthly reports here and—"

He held up a hand, shaking his head. "I have the headache from hell."

She opened her top left desk drawer. "I have some aspirins."

"Aspirins aren't going to help, Sharde. What I need is…" He raked a hand through his hair. "Could we discuss this over dinner?"

"When?"

"Tonight."

"Tonight?" She widened her eyes. "I'd like to Jefferson, but—"

His gaze narrowed and he rose to lean over her desk. He stared into her eyes. "Why are you avoiding me?"

"Avoiding you? I'm not. I—"

"The hell you're not. If I walk into the coffee room, you walk out. If we arrive in the private parking area at the same time, you always manage to linger in your car until I'm inside. If I ask you out for a simple damned meal, you always have other plans!"

Resting his weight on one hand, he curled the fingers of the other hand in her hair, giving it a painful tug. "Don't jerk my chain, Sharde. You're avoiding me and I want to know why."

He was so close she could see the anger in his gray gaze and feel his breath on her lips. She longed to lean forward and kiss the color off his lips. She swallowed instead. "It's the first Friday of the month. I volunteer at the shelter. Remember? You should. We chose it together as a way for company employees to celebrate Martin Luther King Service Day."

"Don't hand me that, Sharde. You're avoiding me." His gaze settled on her cleavage. "And flaunting yourself at the same time."

"Let go of my hair, Jefferson."

He released her hair.

She lifted her chin. "What is it that you want from me?"

He stroked his fingers through her hair and moved closer until his lips were but a breath away. He leaned his body against the desk and stroked the forefinger of his free hand down her chest to come to rest in her cleavage. "I am tired of being teased and denied, Sharde."

His finger seemed to burn into the insides of her breasts. She wet her lips. "We agreed when we left the cabin we'd go back to normal. It was your idea, Jeff. You'd rather have me as a friend than a lover. Remember?"

"I want you."

The muscles in her stomach tightened. "As what?"

He touched his mouth to hers. "I want to sleep with you." He nibbled at her lips, sliding his hand into her blouse to cup her breasts.

She resisted the temptation to lean into him. Instead, she leaned as far back as his fingers in her hair would allow. "And what would happen on Monday? You'd want us to go back to normal?"

He released her hair and cupped his hand on the back of her neck. "We can be friends and lovers," he murmured against her lips.

She drew back, ignoring the ache for his kiss. "We want different things, Jefferson. I'm not interested in a casual relationship that's based solely on sex."

"What do you want it based on?"

"I'm thirty-two and you're thirty-eight. Sex alone doesn't interest me."

"So you're saying. . .what? What it is that you want out of a relationship, Sharde?"

"One of these days I'm going to want to get married and have a couple of kids."

He released his grip on her neck and recoiled as if she'd attempted to strike him. "Marriage? To who?"

She leaned back in her chair, her face flushing. "Clearly not to you."

He stared at her. "Are you seeing anyone?"

She pushed her chair back and rose. "If you're not interested in the meeting, I need some air. It's kind of stuffy in here."

He swung around and turned her to face him. "What do you want me to do, Sharde? Beg? I know the desire isn't all on my side."

She tossed her hair and stared at him. "I'm not interested

in casual, meaningless sex, Jefferson. If I were, I wouldn't seek it from you. Is that clear enough for you?"

He released her, his eyes narrowing. "It's very clear, Sharde."

"So what's it going to be?"

"I'm not in the mood for any shit from you, Sharde." He walked across her office and out the door.

So her wanting anything more than sex from him was shit? Shaking, she went back to her desk and sank down into her seat. Her attempt to force him into something more had backfired. She buttoned her blouse and put her hair back up.

She spent the rest of the day trying without success to concentrate on work. Two hours later, she decided she'd had enough. She picked up her briefcase, the decorative bag containing her new teddy, and walked out her office.

She paused at her secretary's desk. "Judi, I'm going to call it a day. If anything comes up within the next hour that can't wait—"

Judi, fifty-something and mother of several children, gave her a long look. "I'm sure Darbi can handle whatever comes up. You go home and relax."

"I can't. This is my Friday to work at the shelter. I'll see you on Monday."

Judi nodded. "Okay. If you want to talk about it—"

She shook her head. She wasn't about to admit to anyone other than Darbi that she and Jefferson had broken a cardinal rule by sleeping with each other. What was the point when she suspected Judi didn't miss much? "I'll be fine. Thanks. Once I get to the shelter, there'll be so much to do it'll be time to head home to bed before I know it."

She encountered Jefferson in the lobby. "I'm leaving early," she told him. "Have a good weekend."

He nodded curtly and held the entrance door open.

As she went to slip past him, the handle on her lingerie bag caught on one of the brass handles of the door. She heard a tearing sound. She dropped her briefcase and made a grab for the bag. She missed it and the torn bag tumbled to the floor, exposing the dark red teddy.

Before she could bend and grab it and stuff it into her open jacket, Jefferson reached down and picked it up. He stared down at the skimpy material for a long time before he looked at her. "Who are you planning to wear this for?"

Face burning, she snatched it from him, stuffed it inside her coat, picked up her briefcase, and hurried past him into the private parking lot.

She felt a tingle along the back of her neck and turned. Although it was freezing cold and he only wore a suit, he followed her. She paused at her car and faced him. "What is it?"

"You told me you weren't seeing anyone, Sharde."

She opened her car door and tossed her briefcase inside. "It's none of your concern who I see, Jefferson."

"I didn't say it was."

She slid into her car. "Then why the third degree?"

"What third degree? I asked a simple question. If that's too personal for you, forget I asked! Wear it for whoever the hell you like!" He slammed the driver door and quickly walked back towards the building entrance. She sat watching him until he went inside.

Taking several deep breaths, she started her car, and then jumped as someone tapped on her driver side window. She turned and stiffened.

A beautiful blonde with blue eyes bent over her car. Swallowing a rush of dislike, she lowered her window, considering

Vanessa Del Warren with a smile that was as phony as the other woman's. "Vanessa. What brings you here?"

"It's lovely to see you again, Sharde. I'm here to see Jefferson, of course."

"Why?"

Vanessa's smile widened. "Because I want him back. Why else?"

Sharde's nostrils flared. Vanessa would get him back not a moment before hell froze over. "What makes you think that's possible after the way you walked out on him?"

Vanessa flashed her ungloved left hand where she wore a large diamond engagement ring. "He allowed me to keep this ring because he was hoping I'd come back to him. Well, I have."

Bile rose in Sharde's throat. "Things didn't work out in your greener pasture? What's the matter? Frazier wasn't interested?"

Vanessa's eyes shot angry daggers at her. "Look, I've always known you were jealous, but the fact is, Jefferson wants me. He has from the moment we met. I was hoping to enlist your help in getting him back, but now I see you're still consumed by jealousy! I wouldn't waste any more of your time lusting for him, Sharde, because I will have him back!"

"Get the hell out of my face, Vanessa, before I'm tempted to run you over like the road kill you are!"

Vanessa sucked in a breath. "When I have him back under my thumb, the first thing I'm going to do is have you fired."

She laughed. "Wise up, Vanessa. No matter how in love with you he might be, he'd never even consider firing me. You only *think* you know him. I actually know him. Get out of my face—now!"

"Maybe you're right. Maybe he won't fire you. But that just

might suit me better. I think I'm going to enjoy watching you eat your heart out again as I reclaim his heart and this time take his name. How does Vanessa D. Calder sound?"

"Like a pipe dream!"

"Don't you wish?" Vanessa straightened, held her full-length mink around her body, and stalked to the entrance.

Shaken, Sharde sat in her car, uncertain if she should leave as planned or return to work in an effort to ensure Jeff didn't fall into Vanessa's clutches again. She gave an angry shake of her head. If he took her back after she'd left him for Clayton Frazier, they deserved each other.

She drove out of the parking lot to the other side of town. In the shelter's small parking lot, she removed her heels and replaced them with flat shoes. Her wallet, checkbook, and keys went into the leather fanny pack she fastened around her waist, under her jacket. Getting out of the car, she locked her briefcase, handbag, and the teddy in the trunk of her car before going into the big rundown building where she spent the first Friday of the month volunteering.

She went in through the back entrance. A tall, thin woman with faded blonde hair and brown eyes stood behind a table serving a group of men and women. She looked up, her smile rearranging the lines around her mouth. "Sharde. You're early."

Sharde hung her outside and suit jackets on a clothes tree and donned one of two aprons hanging there. She moved behind the table and reached for the ladle. "You look like you could use a break, Dianne. Why don't you go home early? I'll finish serving, give out condoms if anyone comes asking, and lock up before I go."

Dianne sighed, surrendering the ladle. "I wish I could, but state funding has been cut again and I have to go crunch numbers and see where and how we can go on."

Sharde had been volunteering at the All Faiths House for the last five years. Although most company employees only volunteered during the month of January, both Sharde and Jefferson volunteered monthly. She came every first Friday of the month and she knew that Jefferson, whose hobby was carpentry, often came to make repairs to the building since the place always seemed a breath away from falling down.

"Go home, Dianne. I'll crunch the numbers for you and leave you a note on your desk."

"I couldn't ask you to do that. It will take hours."

She shrugged, lading several ladles full of fragrant beef stew into the bowl of the man standing in front of her. "It's not like I have anything pressing to do."

Dianne hesitated. "Are you sure? I am tired, but I hate to impose on you."

Keeping busy would help take her mind off what might be happening with Jeff and Vanessa. She shook her head. "It's no imposition. I can sleep late tomorrow, but you'll be back here doing breakfast. Just this once, take yourself home to Arthur early." She grinned. "There's no use in both of us going dateless on a Friday night."

"Okay. You twisted my arm." She gave Sharde's free hand a squeeze and hurried along the back of the room to the door leading into the office.

Two hours later, the last of the diners left the large dining room. Sharde sighed and put the ladle down. Taking off her apron, she started across the room to lock the door.

She was halfway there when the door swung open. She bit back a tired sigh. If it was more than one person there was not going to be enough stew. "You're a little late, but come on..."

Jefferson entered.

A wave of relief washed over her. He wasn't somewhere lying in bed with Vanessa allowing her to reel him back in. She frowned. The faithless hussy could be waiting in his car for all she knew.

He looked around the large room, then turned and locked the door. "Where's Dianne?"

"I sent her home. What are you doing here?"

He lifted a large metal tool case. "I promised her I'd fix the doors to the women's bathroom."

Although there were no beds, the homeless were welcome to shower and hand wash their personal items every morning except Sunday when the shelter part of the store front church didn't open until two p.m. for an early dinner. "Oh."

She bit back the urge to ask him about Vanessa. She'd probably given up that right when she refused to sleep with him again. Besides, Vanessa wasn't the kind to sit quietly in the car. "Well. . .you know the way."

He nodded and made his way across the back of the dining room. She went around the dining room gathering the plates and utensils. Many of the plates were chipped, but Dianne insisted the shelter use china and silver instead of paper plates and plastic utensils.

She pushed the dish cart down the hall to the kitchen. She loaded the dishes into the dishwashers and left the kitchen. Walking down the hall to the office, she could hear Jefferson's electric screwdriver buzzing.

She went into the office and sat behind Dianne's battered desk. She looked at all the receipts and folders, sighed, and turned on the calculator. As she worked, the sounds of Jeff's tools provided surprisingly pleasant background ambiance.

An hour and a half later, she finished and sat back, rotating her shoulders. The shelter really needed a steady source of income instead of depending on monthly allotments from the state that were frequently cut.

She took out her checkbook, wrote out a check to the shelter to cover the shortfall, and rose. Making her way through the quiet building, she realized she hadn't heard Jeff's tools for some time.

A dim, forty-watt bulb provided the only illumination of the long corridor she had to traverse to reach the exit. Anxious to get out of the empty building and get home to a tossed salad and bed, she quickened her pace.

As she passed the women's shower room, the door swung silently open. Frightened, she stumbled backwards until she saw Jeff. Her shoulders sagged and she gave him an angry look. "You scared me witless!"

"Did I? Let me make it up to you."

"What?"

Closing his hands on her arms, he pulled her against him. His mouth crashed down on hers, swallowing any protest she might have made.

With thoughts of Vanessa waiting in the wings to win him back, she abandoned any thoughts of playing hard to get. She shuddered and melted against him. It had only been three weeks since they'd spent three and a half days in each other's arms, but it seemed as if it had been an eternity.

She clung to him, immersing herself in the pleasure of his mouth moving so hungrily over hers as he crushed her in his arms. She loved everything about him, from the taste of his mouth, the feel of his aroused body against hers, the sound of his voice, husky with desire, to the absolute joy of knowing she could arouse deep-rooted passion in him.

Still devouring her lips, he turned her, easing her back until she came to a stop against the wall beside the door.

The fanny pack around her waist bit into her stomach, impeding the level of intimacy they could achieve. He reached around her back and unbuckled it. He pulled it from between their bodies, dropped it to the floor near their feet, and pressed his body tight against hers.

She knew she should stop him. After all, she'd just told him that afternoon that she didn't want meaningless sex. But she ached for him and couldn't deny either of them. Besides, if she didn't give him what he so clearly needed, he might go to Vanessa. And damn if she'd allow Vanessa to get her hooks into him again. Even if things didn't work out between her and Jefferson, he deserved better than Vanessa.

She raised her hands to his back to hold him as she returned the heat and fierceness of his kiss, parting her lips so that their tongues could tangle and dance together.

Passion and desire raged in her. He pulled the pins from her hair, tugging uncomfortably in his eagerness to free it. When her hair fell around her cheeks and shoulders, he buried his face in it, holding her tight, pressing her against the wall as he ground himself against her.

"Sharde...?"

She felt the unmistakable bulge between his legs against her. Recalling the sweet interlude at the cabin, her knees shook and she went damp. Damp, hungry and a little crazy. She had to have him.

Shaking with need, she pushed him away and tugged at her clothes. He took her hand and led her into the shower room and beyond to the bathroom. Unzipping his pants, he sat down on the highest toilet seat. He reached into his open trousers and drew out his cock.

Her mouth went dry as he sat with his legs parted, his fully erect shaft protruding from within his pants. Heart hammering and her core damp with love and lust, she pushed up her skirt, yanked down her panties and pantyhose. She kicked off one shoe, pulling the pantyhose over that leg and foot. Leaving the other part of her panty hose on just below her knee, she straddled his body, her eyes on the cock she couldn't wait to feel invading her body again.

He dug in his jacket pocket and handed her a condom. She took it and pushed it in his shirt pocket.

She moved to sit on him, but his strong hands on her waist halted her downward movement with his cock just a heartbeat from her entrance. "It's crazy to do this again without a condom."

"We've already been through this, Jeff! We don't need to rehash it."

"Neither one of us was thinking clearly at the cabin."

"And you're thinking clearly now?"

"Enough to know that we should use a condom."

"I want to feel you inside me...not a piece of latex. And I want you to come inside me."

He shook his head. "Sharde—"

"What are you afraid of?"

"I'm not afraid of anything except hurting you."

"I'm a big girl. I can take care of myself and I know what I want and I want you inside me now. We're both clean and I'm protected against pregnancy. So no condom." She stared at him, her frustration building. "Or maybe you'd rather have Vanessa?"

"Fuck Vanessa!"

"Have you been fucking her tonight?"

"Hell, no! You think I'm that stupid? The only woman I'm going to fuck tonight is you, you teasing bitch!" He jerked down on her waist. She reached between their legs, curled her fingers around his thick, hot length, and lowered her hips, facing him. She wiggled her hips, driving his bare cock deep up into her body.

She straddled him, with her legs on either side of his thighs. "Oh." She sighed with pleasure as the last few inches of his thickness slid into her body. She sat with her lips parted, her eyes glazed, luxuriating in the wonderfully full feeling that she'd never experienced with anyone else. Lord, there was nothing quite as delicious as his thick, long cock.

Whoever said white men had small cocks clearly had never met Jeff and his pussy-stretching cock. Lord, it felt good...so good. "Oooh."

He moved his hands from her hips and pulled her blouse open. The silk fabric tore and buttons flew everywhere. The blouse had cost a small fortune, but she was too far gone to care about anything but what was about to happen. He reached around her body and unhooked her bra. Feeling wanton, she shook her upper body and her breasts bounced into view.

He didn't spend any time looking or fondling. He groaned softly, leaned forward, and closed his lips over her right breast, his tongue teasing the nipple.

She moaned and rotated her butt against his thighs, loving the way his mouth felt on her breasts and the way his cock jerked inside her.

She linked her arms around his neck and slowly lifted and lowered her hips. Each time she sat down on his lap, he thrust his hips upward, burying himself deep inside her slick center of need. Joy radiated all through her and she thought she would lose her mind.

Sex had never been this good...this wonderful...this fulfilling with any other lover. Her feelings for him left her feeling raw and open to hurt. But for this incredible, delicious delight, she was willing to risk getting hurt.

He sucked at her breasts until they felt almost unbearably tender. She clasped her hands over his face, pulled his head up, and pressed her lips over his.

Kissing him deeply, she thrust her tongue into his mouth. She stroked her fingers through his soft, silky hair, sliding up and down on his long, throbbing length with a greedy enjoyment that nearly robbed her of her ability to breathe.

Her heightened senses urged her to seek greater pleasure. The passion and the delight tightened her stomach muscles. She gasped against his lips, riding him faster.

He groaned, grabbed her hips, and slammed her up and down onto his heated flesh with a fury that sent her over the edge of a high cliff and tumbling down into the valley of bliss. Her pussy squeezed and tightened uncontrollably around his cock until he thrust into her, hurting her.

It was such a sweet pain. It prolonged her pleasure. When he came, calling out her name and blasting his seed deep inside her, she smiled and cradled him against her breasts, squeezing her pussy around his cock to milk the last drop of seed from him.

Finally, she collapsed against him, sucking his neck while he continued coming in her, putting out the fire his cock had started inside her.

She laid her face against his shoulder. He held her close, stroking his hands down her body until she stopped shaking. As she lay in his arms, feeling weak and satisfied, he pulled back, lifted her chin, and pressed a long, warm kiss against her mouth.

He bit into her bottom lip and slapped her on both cheeks,

making them sting. "Holy hell, Sharde, each time with you is better than the time before."

She lifted her head and looked at him. "That was good enough to make me wanna holler," she told him.

He laughed and rewarded her with another set of stinging slaps against her behind. He moved his hands over her butt. "You have a lovely ass," he told her. He looked directly into her eyes. "I'll bet it would look so sexy all red with a palm print or two branding it and you as mine."

Sitting on his lap with his semi-erect shaft still inside her soaked pussy, the sexy words made her gasp. "I've never…no one's ever hit me there before."

"Your ass was made for spanking," he told her, slapping each cheek again. "Not to mention fucking."

She shook her head. He wasn't getting his cock anywhere near her ass until he was prepared to commit to her. But the mere thought of him spanking her? Well, that intrigued her. "I thought only bad girls were spanked. I haven't been bad," she whispered. She had never really engaged in anything but vanilla sex, but she had a feeling she'd enjoy nearly anything Jefferson wanted to do to her.

He leered at her, his gray eyes dancing. "You call having sex in a bathroom on the toilet being good?" Before she could answer, he slapped her left ass cheek.

Cheeks hot, she nevertheless gave him a wanton smile. "It felt very good and you were the one who dragged me in here and had your wicked way with me."

"And how does this feel?" He slapped her cheek again, this time hard enough to make it sting.

She shuddered and her pussy tightened around his cock. "Oooh. That hurt."

"Did it?" He brought his palm down against her cheek. "How about that?"

She caught her breath as her cheek tingled. "That hurt too!" she whispered in a breathless, excited voice.

"Then why do you sound so excited?"

Sitting on his lap with his cock still inside her, she felt wanton, sexy, and hungry to feel his palm stinging her ass cheeks. "Because I'm a bad girl?"

"Oh, you've been a very bad girl." He slapped her ass again, several times in quick succession. She moaned and thrust her breasts against his chest. His cock, still inside her, hardened. She leaned against him, slowly rotating herself on his lap.

"Then you'd better punish me."

"Oh, baby, I intend to!" Lifting her hips, he brought her back down, thrusting his hips upward.

As his cock shot up into her, she cupped her hands over her breasts and arched her back. "Ooooh. Punish me, Jeff!"

Holding her with one arm around her waist, he fucked her slowly. He slapped her cheeks each time he thrust his cock back into her. The combination of his hard cock pumping in and out of her and his palm delivering those delicious, stingy blows sent her over the edge. Within minutes, she cried out, curled her fingers in his hair, sucked his tongue into her mouth and blew apart.

She collapsed against him, sobbing softly as her climax washed over her. Cupping his palms over her stinging cheeks, he bit into her shoulder, shuddered, and came.

For several moments, they clung to each other, and then he caressed her ass. "I'm going to want this the next time," he whispered.

After the sweet heat of what they'd just shared, she was no longer sure she wanted to make him wait until he was ready to commit to her before she agreed to anal sex with him. The thought of his cock sliding between her cheeks and deep inside her ass sent a thrill of lust through her. They could both kneel on all fours. He could lean over her back with one big hand over her breasts while the fingers of his other hand dug in her pussy or played with her clit. Oh, hell, that would be so good. She moistened her lips and hoped she didn't sound breathless when she spoke. "We'll see."

"Yes, we will." He slapped her ass lightly, kissed her briefly, and then moved his hands to her hips, lifting her off him. When she stood up, her knees knocked and she had to lean against him for a moment. He rose and turned to draw her into his arms. "Don't make me wait too long." He stroked his palms gently over her bottom. "It's been a very long time since I met a woman with an ass that begged to be fucked as yours does."

Did that mean he and Vanessa had never had anal sex? She smiled up at him, linking her arms around his neck. "My cheeks hurt."

He turned her around, bent, and pressed several soft kisses against her bottom. He straightened and turned her back to face him. "Better?"

She had loved feeling his mouth moving on her ass. She smiled. "Yes."

He kissed her nose. "Good, but you'd better get used to having them sting after we make love."

"If you think I'm going to have you beating my ass every time—"

He pressed a finger against her lips. "Not beating your ass. Spanking it during lovemaking. There's a big difference between the two."

She nodded. "I didn't mean beating it in a bad way."

"Good." He pinched her nipples. "They'd look awfully cute with nipple rings attached."

"Nipple rings? Are you into—"

"I'm into you. And I'm eager to explore every possible way of making love to and with you, Sharde." He stroked her cheek. "Does the thought frighten or turn you off?"

She shook her head. "I can't imagine anything you'd want to do to and with me during lovemaking turning me off."

He smiled and palmed her ass again. "Then this is going to belong to me soon."

She didn't deny it.

"Now I'm starving. Let's go find something to eat. Then we need to talk."

CHAPTER SIX

"Talk?" She withdrew her arms from his neck. "What about?"

"About when you're going to introduce me to your sweet ass...and other things."

"What other things?

He stroked a finger down her cheek. "Sharde, we can't pretend this didn't happen. We have to talk about it."

"Why? Nothing's changed for me. Has anything changed for you?"

Her voice sounded needy, almost desperate. She bit her bottom lip.

"Things changed for me the moment we took that tumble in the snow."

She moved against the wall and struggled to pull on her pantyhose. He surprised her by getting her shoe and then kneeling. She put a hand on his shoulder and extended her feet. Before sliding her shoe on, he lifted her pantyhose-clad foot. He pressed a kiss against the sole of her foot before sliding on her shoe.

He reached into her ruined blouse and pulled her bra down. Looking down into her eyes, he managed to fasten it. He stepped back from her, considering her blouse.

She looked down at it and up at him. "This is ruined. Do you know how much this blouse cost?"

He steadied it for several moments before speaking. "About two, three hundred dollars."

"It cost two-fifty. How did you guess so accurately?"

He shrugged, his eyes narrowing. "Before she decided I couldn't afford her, Linda did her best to spend me into the poorhouse."

He sounded bitter and she sighed. Would he ever get over the hurt the other two women had inflicted on him? "And Vanessa?"

"What about her?"

"What happened when you...did you see her after I left the office?"

"Yes."

"And? What happened?"

"Nothing happened. I told her I had no interest in allowing her to make a fool of me for a second time."

"And?"

"And she whipped off her mink to reveal nothing but a pair of stockings and heels. She offered to allow me to fuck her ass."

What man could resist such an invitation? She moistened her lips. "And?"

"And I told her thanks, but no thanks. I was tempted to tell her why her skinny little ass no longer interested me, but I didn't think you'd appreciate her knowing I have carnal designs on your beautiful brown ass."

She blushed with pleasure and excitement. "So...it's over between you for good?"

"Yes!"

"So you don't expect to see her again?"

"Oh, I'm fairly sure she'll surface again. She's not the kind to easily admit defeat, but sooner or later she'll have to realize that once with her was enough to last me a lifetime."

"Oh, good. When I saw her and she told me…I was afraid you still had feelings for her."

"I do, but none of them are the warm and fuzzy kind she was hoping for."

"You were so in love with her. I—"

"I was in lust with her. Not in love. There's a difference between the two, Sharde. I was in big time lust with her, but any lingering desire I felt for her vanished the first time you and I made love."

Made love? Or had sex? It had been love for her. She knew he didn't view her as just an easy lay, but she doubted if he were in love with her—yet.

"Now." He took off his jacket and slipped it around her shoulders. "Let's go eat."

She looked at him; his shaft, now soft but still surprisingly impressive, hung out of his pants. She palmed him, squeezing him gently as she pushed his flesh back inside his pants and briefs. She slid his zipper up and was rewarded with a quick kiss.

They washed their hands before he took her hand and led her back out into the hall. He stopped to pick up her fanny pack. He fastened it and slid it over his shoulder. In the dining room, she slipped her outer jacket on over his jacket.

They made a quick circuit around the building to ensure that everything was secured, set the alarm, and left.

They walked hand in hand to her car. He nodded to his SUV. "Let's take mine. I'll drive you back tomorrow to get your car."

That implied he expected them to spend the night together. "I'd love to ride with you, but Dianne will worry if she arrives tomorrow and finds my car still here. I'd better drive it myself."

He handed over her fanny pack. "Where do you want to eat?"

Considering they must both smell like sex, their options were limited. "I could do a few steaks with some stir-fry vegetables if you want to come back to my place."

"Got a beer?"

She arched a brow. "When don't I keep a six-pack around just for you?"

"Small wonder I'm nuts about you." He leaned down and kissed her. "I'll follow you."

***

At her condo, she changed into a pink silk pantsuit that hugged all her curves. When she emerged from her bathroom, he leered at her and let loose a wolf whistle. She smiled as he followed her into the kitchen. Seated at the table there, he watched as she prepared their meal. When she set his plate and a beer in front of him, he pulled her down onto his lap, nuzzling her neck. "We can share this," he whispered.

She shivered, trying to decide if she wanted to eat him or food.

He unbuttoned her blouse and unhooked her bra, freeing her breasts. He turned her on his lap and buried his face against her.

She smiled. "Hmmm…"

He kissed and sucked each mound. She closed her eyes, loving the feel of his cock hardening against her butt. She pressed down, and then pulled away, jerking off his lap.

He let her go, but locked his gaze on her. "What's wrong?"

She refastened her bra and buttoned her blouse. "You said you were hungry."

He took a sip of his beer. "When I'm around you my chief hunger is not for food."

She fixed her plate, poured herself a glass of her favorite red wine and sat opposite him. "You were right, Jeff. This sleeping with each other is not a good idea. We can't pretend we're just colleagues while at work and then go sneaking around after hours."

He cut his steak and speared a chunk. He chewed it slowly, a look of enjoyment on his face. He took another sip of his beer and looked at her. "Why not? We're not married or committed to anyone else. And it's not sneaking around. We just won't advertise our relationship in the office."

She cut a piece of steak and pushed it around her plate. "I told you I'm not interested in a strictly sexual relationship. I need to think about my future."

He put his knife and fork down, arching a brow. "Sharde, we've slept together a few times. Surely you're not looking for a marriage proposal already."

She stared down at her plate, tears stinging her eyes. He had proposed to Vanessa after one weekend. But despite his earlier insistence he'd been in lust instead of love, Sharde was convinced he had been in love with the beautiful blonde. Lust was clearly all Sharde could expect.

"A marriage proposal from you? No. I know you only fall for beautiful, faithless blondes." She looked up at him. "That sort of leaves me out on three counts, doesn't it?"

He sat back in his seat, staring at her. "Are we back to race, Sharde?"

"Did we ever really leave race, Jefferson?"

"I did. It was never an issue with me."

"Then tell me why I shouldn't expect anything but sex when beautiful, blonde, white Vanessa got a marriage proposal after one weekend of shaking her skinny ass at you. Tell me, did she allow you to spank and fuck that skinny ass of hers?"

He sucked in an angry breath. "I'm telling you for the last damn time that race has nothing to do with this, Sharde! Nothing."

"Really? Then what is this all about?"

"How can you believe I think less of you than I did of her? Even if you were a white blonde, I'm not interested in or ready for another serious relationship. That's no reflection on the color of your hair or your skin. You should know by now how sexually attracted I am to you."

"Then what's this all about?"

"Just what I said. I am just not emotionally ready to risk my heart again."

She couldn't help noticing how he deliberately ignored mentioning her looks. She moistened her lips. "Okay. Fair enough. You're not interested in anything serious and I'm not interested in anything but a serious relationship. I think that sort of says it all, Jeff."

He raked a hand through his hair. "You can talk all you want about serious relationships, but you can't deny that you want me as much as I want you. And you can't deny that what we share is special and worth taking the time to get it right. While we do that, what's wrong with us satisfying our hungers with each other?"

Because her chief hunger wasn't for sex with him, it was for his love. It was finally clear to her that she had no hope of winning that. That only left the question of how much less she would be willing to settle for.

When she had set out on her mission of conquest, she had been willing to settle for his lust. She had been able to arouse his passions in a way she had never thought possible. Could she learn to be satisfied with just the lust of a man she loved so much she ached for him?

She recalled his hunger for her and a small flicker of hope ignited inside her. Would he really have such a deep desire for her if there were no chance of his ever feeling anything else?

She decided to try one last tactic before she gave up. "Okay. You're right. I can't deny I want you. So here's what we'll do. We'll go on as we are now, but if either of us meets someone else, all bets are off."

"Someone else? What do you mean? Another man?"

She arched a brow. "I don't do women, Jefferson. Yes. Another man for me and a woman for you."

"You're telling me there's a possibility you'll be sleeping with me and another man at the same time?"

She noted the tightening of his lips and the edge to his voice. She had no intentions of sleeping with anyone else. But he didn't need to know that. "Don't worry. From here on out, I'll use protection. You promise to do the same and we have a deal." She extended her hand across the table. "Shake on it?"

He ignored her hand. "You must be mixing me up with one of your other boyfriends. I don't sleep with more than one woman at a time, Sharde."

"Fine." She withdrew her hand and picked up her fork. "If you're not interested in a serious relationship you can't expect me to agree to restrictive clauses. I have to keep my options open."

She smiled at him and popped a forkful of steak into her mouth. She chewed and swallowed without tasting it.

"You have to keep your options open?" He pushed his plate away. "If you think I'm going to stick around while you bed another man—"

"Why should it matter to you what I do as long as I'm careful? Sex with you is the best I've ever had. But if I meet a man who wants a serious relationship, but might not possess your skill as a lover, if I can convince him to share, why should that bother you?"

He slammed a fist down on the table and shot to his feet. "Are you out of your mind, Sharde? Do you really think after what I went through with Linda and Vanessa I could ever be persuaded to share you with another man?"

She lifted her chin. "Why not? I understand why you couldn't share them...you were in love with both of them."

"I was not in love with Vanessa."

"Then she and I are in the same boat...we're just the object of your lust."

"It's not just lust between us! How can you think it is?"

"You haven't given me any reason to think differently, Jefferson."

"You are out of your tiny little mind if you think for one moment I'll share you with another man."

Her heart raced. She shrugged, taking another mouthful of food before she looked up at him. "Then we can go back to plan A."

"And what the hell is plan A?"

"Friendship with no sex. You only have two choices. I can live with either one you choose."

He leaned across the table and glared at her. "I do not share my woman."

"I'm not your woman. I'm just your current booty call."

He recoiled. "I never treated you like any damned booty call, Sharde!"

"Oh, I don't know, Jefferson. I'm willing to bet you never pulled either Linda or Vanessa into a shower of a shelter and took them on the toilet. I'm certain you never told either one of them their ass would look good red and branded with your palm prints."

He raked a hand through his hair. "I...this is not about either of them."

"Of course it is. They hurt you and everyone else has to pay the price for their infidelity."

He leveled a finger at her. "You don't have to pay the price for anything, Sharde. But hell will freeze over before I allow another woman—even you—to manipulate me!"

"Then where does this leave us?"

"I'll tell you where it leaves us! You know those two choices you mentioned? I'll take plan A...no sex."

Her heart felt as if it was being ripped into little pieces. But she was determined not to reveal how much his words hurt. "Fine. I can live without having sex with you."

"You fickle little...bitch! Not two hours past you were insisting I do you without a condom."

"Do me?!"

"Yes, Sharde, *do* you! I *did* you...without a condom, at your insistence, and now you think I'm going to allow you to jerk me around? Hell, no! You want to play damned games? You go fuck whoever the hell you like and see if I care!"

She swallowed hard to dislodge a lump of misery. "Jeff—"

"Fuck off, Sharde!"

He turned and stormed out of the kitchen. When he left, he slammed her apartment door so violently she jumped. The tears stinging her eyes fell unchecked down her cheeks.

Determined not to spend a sleepless night crying in her pillow for him, she finished half the bottle of wine. Feeling groggy and miserable, she put her plate and Jefferson's in the refrigerator and stumbled down the hall to her bedroom.

She undressed and fell face down across the bed. She

hugged the pillow close, closed her eyes, whispered Jefferson's name, and fell asleep.

***

Jefferson sat in his SUV outside of Sharde's building, taking slow, deep breaths in an effort to calm the emotions raging in him. What was wrong with him that he kept attracting the wrong type of woman?

He looked up at the building. Sharde was the last woman he'd expected to take fidelity so lightly. How could she be so uninhibited…hell…wanton with him and then casually expect him to share her with another man?

It was unreasonable of her to expect him to be ready for anything serious so soon after Vanessa's infidelity. Did she think he had no feelings? There was still an ache inside him left by the two women he had unwisely given possession of his heart. Why couldn't she understand that it would take time before he felt ready to trust his heart to another woman? Didn't she know that when he was ready, she'd be that woman?

Just because he wasn't ready or able to entrust his heart to her immediately didn't mean he would have been anything but faithful to her. He clenched his fists around the steering wheel, bile rising in his gut as he thought of Sharde sleeping with another man. He had thought of little except her since their weekend at the cabin. How could something that meant so much to him mean so little to her?

He closed his eyes and pressed his forehead against the steering wheel. He was hurt and furious that she could so easily choose to abandon the physical relationship that he ached for with her.

He sat up, casting a final look up at her building. What would she say if he went back and accepted her offer? He gave an angry shake of his head. He was not going back. Damn if he'd allow another damned faithless woman to jerk his chain. She wanted other men. She could damn well have as many of them as she could handle, but he would not be one of them. And two could play her damn game.

He had not expected to feel this anguish and pain in his gut and heart again. Damn her. He started his SUV. He drove home, undressed, showered, and dressed in casual trousers and a pullover.

After dressing, he called Ben.

"I hope this is important."

Ben's voice was low and annoyed. Jefferson frowned. "Did I catch you at a bad time?"

"Yes. What is it?"

"I need to talk."

Ben didn't sound very best friend like. "Can't you talk to Sharde?"

"No, I can't! She's the damned problem."

There was a brief pause before Ben spoke again. "I see. So how long have you been sleeping with her?"

"I'm not sleeping with her!" he snapped, annoyed that Ben seemed to be implying Sharde was easy.

"Good! Then go talk and to her because I am in the middle of a date with a very...interesting woman. She's in the powder room." He sighed. "If you really need me, I'll risk blue balls and send her home."

Just because he would be spending the night alone didn't mean Ben should as well. "No. Sorry to interrupt. I'll talk to you later."

"You're angry, but otherwise all right?"

He was angry and hurt. He wasn't sure which emotion was

stronger. "I'll be fine. I'll talk to you tomorrow," he said and hung up.

Snatching his vehicle keys, he got back in his SUV and drove along the highway until he spotted a bar in an upscale neighborhood.

He pulled into the parking lot and strolled inside. He stood in the doorway, looking around. His glance settled on a pretty brunette and a slender blonde, both of who seemed to be alone. Remembering Sharde's taunt about how he only fell for faithless blondes, he made his way over to the brunette.

"Hi."

She looked up and smiled. She had pretty brown eyes…almost as deep as Sharde's. "Hi."

Hell, she even sounded a little like Sharde. Her hair was dark and almost as glossy as Sharde's. "Can I buy you a drink?"

Her smile widened. "Yes. Yes you can."

He looked down into eyes. Damn if he'd spend another long, lonely night hungering for Sharde. If she wanted to play games, she could play alone.

He smiled at the brunette and slipped onto the stool beside her.

CHAPTER SEVEN

Sharde woke in the middle of the night with the certainty that after being hurt by two women in such a short time, it was unreasonable of her to expect too much from Jeff too soon.

He needed time to get over his hurts and then more time to realize that she would not hurt him. She had not helped her cause by suggesting she would sleep with him and another man at the same time. She hadn't meant a word of that nonsense, but how could she ever convince him of that now?

Deciding that morning was too long to make right what she'd messed up, she sat up in bed and dialed his number. She glanced at her bedside clock. It was just after two a.m. If he hadn't had too many beers, maybe he would come over and they'd spend the rest of the night making up.

Just as she was about to hang up, the phone was picked up on the sixth ring. "Hello?"

Sharde stiffened before realizing she'd dialed the wrong number. "I'm so sorry. Wrong number," she said and hung up. She dialed again, making sure she dialed correctly this time.

"Hello?"

A woman's voice again and this time she knew she'd dialed the correct number. "I'm sorry. I was looking for Jefferson."

"He's asleep. Do you want me to wake him?"

She had problems speaking past the lump in her throat. "No. I'm sorry I disturbed you."

"Look, you're not his wife are you? Because he told me he was divorced."

"I'm…nobody." She hung up the phone, and then took it off the hook. She lay staring up at the ceiling for what seemed hours, tears steaming down her cheeks before she got up, went into the kitchen, and finished the bottle of wine.

***

"Are you feeling better?"

Sprawled on his bed on his face, Jefferson froze. He knew he was home. And he knew the female voice did not belong to Sharde. Oh, shit. What the hell had he done? He lifted his head and rolled onto his back.

A tall, pretty brunette leaned over him, a smile dancing in her dark brown eyes. "Earth to Jefferson. You in there?"

He ran his hands over his body and was relieved to find himself fully dressed. He sat up. "Who are you?"

She laughed and shook her head. "The next time I allow a man to pick me up in a bar, I'll make sure he can deliver."

"What?"

Her eyes narrowed. "You are all show and no go. You couldn't get it up last night. I don't blame you for pretending you can't remember what happened…or should I say, didn't happen?"

He frowned. "Are you saying that I…didn't…"

"I'm saying you couldn't get it up. Next time you pick up a woman, don't drink so much."

His face burned. "I've never been unable to perform."

"No? Well take it from me, your libido was a no-show last night."

"So you and I…didn't sleep together?"

"That's about all we did do…sleep in the same bed. As I said, you couldn't get it up. I didn't even get a decent kiss from you. I suppose you do know how to kiss properly when you're not too drunk to get it up."

He closed his eyes. Thank God he hadn't slept with her, but what the hell had possessed him to bring her home? That argument with Sharde had really put him in a bad emotional state. For all her talk of their each taking other lovers, he feared Sharde would find his taking another woman home unforgivable.

"Look, I've wasted enough time with you. You want to get up and give me a ride home or at the very least cab fare?"

He got up and reached in his back pocket for his wallet. He gave her several twenty-dollar bills. "Look I'm sorry about last night. I shouldn't have brought you here."

"I shouldn't have come with you." She touched his cheek. "But you are one handsome devil. A pity you're impotent!"

"I am not impotent!"

"You were last night." She laughed, grabbed a long dark coat from the chair by the bed and headed for the bedroom door. There she turned back to look at him. "And next time you're cheating on your wife, be more discreet."

"I'm not married."

"That's what you told me last night, but someone called here twice after two in the morning. She sounded very upset when I answered. If she wasn't your wife, she must have been your girlfriend."

He closed his eyes briefly. *Oh, God! Please let it have been Vanessa and not Sharde.* "What was her name?"

She shrugged. "She didn't say and I didn't ask, but she sounded like a hot to trot sista. Like to play jungle fever, huh?"

He gave her a cold, silent stare.

She shrugged and left him alone in his bedroom.

He lay on his back, staring up at the ceiling for several

moments. Why the hell hadn't he kept his ass home the night before? Had he done that he and Sharde could have talked after they'd both had time to cool off. But he couldn't undo the night before. And lying there wasn't going to change anything. He'd have to admit he'd taken another woman home, ride out her angry outburst, and do whatever was necessary to make things right with her.

Of course it was possible, albeit not very probable, that Sharde had not called. He rolled over and off the bed. He walked over to his phone and looked down at the phone number of the last person who had called. Sharde's number was listed twice, less than a minute apart.

He was screwed.

***

Sharde woke late the next morning. Her head ached and she felt dizzy and nauseous. Holding her head, she stumbled to the kitchen to down a twenty-ounce bottle of ginger ale. She followed with a cold shower and coffee. By the time she dressed, she felt almost human again.

She boiled two eggs, ate them, grabbed her keys, and left her condo. She didn't allow her thoughts to dwell on Jefferson, their confrontation of the night before, or the fact that he had gone out and found someone to spend the night with. He had made his choice and she needed to make hers.

As she pulled into the shelter parking lot, she decided that she would give a month's notice on Monday. It was time to face reality and move on. Jefferson was never going to feel anything but lust for her. And even that hadn't kept him from going to another woman the same night he'd had sex with her.

Dianne looked up in surprise when she walked into the

shelter. "I didn't expect to see you today, Sharde. Thanks so much for the check."

"It was my pleasure."

Dianne studied her face. "Is everything all right?"

She shook her head. Everything was wrong. "No, but I don't want to talk about it. I just need to be kept really busy. I don't want to have time to think. Can I stay?"

"Of course you can. We always need at least three more pairs of hands around here. Grab an apron and help me serve lunch."

"What would you say if I asked to come work here for a while?"

Dianne paused in ladling up chicken soup to look at her. "You mean more than once every first Friday of the month? That would be great. How often do you want to come? Twice a month? How about the first and third Fridays of the month? Or did you want to change to another night?"

Sharde put a roll on the tray of the man to whom Dianne had just given soup. "Actually I was thinking more like five times a week."

Dianne glanced at her and went back to ladling soup. "What's wrong, Sharde?"

"Nothing."

"Sharde?"

She shrugged. "Nothing I can't handle."

"And that would be?"

"I'm resigning from Calder Tech on Monday."

"Why?"

She shrugged again. "Personal reasons."

"Have you talked this over with Jefferson?"

"He's the last person I can discuss this with."

Dianne gave her arm a brief squeeze. "If you need to talk…"

"I'm fine. Really. Don't worry. I have everything worked out in my mind. This is something I should have done a few years ago."

"Is there anything I can do to help?"

"Yes. I've decided to take a few weeks off before I look for another job. In the meantime, I want to do something useful and not just sit around feeling sorry for myself."

"It's Jefferson, isn't it?"

"What…what do you mean?" She had never discussed her feelings for Jefferson with Dianne.

"I know you have feelings for him. I saw it every time the two of you came here to volunteer. What's happened between you two?"

She shook her head. "I appreciate your kindness, but I can't talk about it. Can I…come here five times a week in about a month's time?"

"Of course you can, Sharde, but wouldn't it be better to try and work things out with him?"

"No. There's nothing to work out."

Dianne sighed. "If you change your mind and need or want to talk, I'll be available any time of the day or night."

"Thanks."

Two hours later, Sharde sat over a late lunch with Darbi at a food court in a mall fifteen minutes from All Faiths.

"You don't think resigning is too drastic, Sharde?"

She shook her head. "I can't work with him anymore."

"This is a bad time to leave."

"I know. I'll stay until the decisions on hiring new employees have been made and other administrative matters handled."

"And after that?"

"You'll be back from your trip and can handle things. You're as capable of doing my job as I am...which is one of the reasons I hired you."

She nodded. "I think so too, but I like the travel my job entails and yours doesn't permit. Besides, I think you'd be foolish to give up such a prestigious position, Sharde. Why not take a leave, transfer to the uptown branch, and stay with the company?"

She shook her head. "Even if I transferred, I'd still have to have a certain level of interaction with him. That's the last thing I want. I need to get away from him and everything he stands for."

"I know this is difficult for you, but Sharde, don't you think you're overreacting just a little? You know I understand about infidelity, but let's just take a moment and step back from the situation. All he said was he wasn't ready for a serious commitment. Given his recent history, surely you can understand his reluctance."

"I do understand, but at the same time I feel as if I've wasted all the time I'm going to waste with him. It's time to move on."

"Sharde, look. We're friends and so I'm going to give it to you straight."

She frowned. "This sounds like something I'm not going to like."

"Friends are straight with each other."

"Okay. Give it to me straight then."

"Given your remarks about another lover, I think you're overreacting."

Her cheeks burned. "I didn't mean it and I know he knew that. He just wanted an excuse for hopping into bed with yet another blonde bimbo!"

"How do you know she was blonde and a bimbo?"

MARILYN LEE

"I know because that's the only kind of women he admires!"

"Look, I can see your pain, but you know he admires you."

"It's not his admiration I want or need. I want more than he's prepared to give me so it's time to move on."

"Without giving him a chance to explain?"

"What's to explain? He took another woman to bed the same night he and I..." She blinked rapidly to keep her tears at bay. "The same night, Darbi. There's no explanation he can offer that will make that forgivable for me."

Darbi sighed. "OK. If you need to talk more..."

She shook her head. "Thanks, but it's time to keep it real and move on." She glanced at her watch. "I'd better get back to All Faiths. I told Dianne I'd cover so she could go home early."

She spent the rest of the day and evening at the shelter. After the last meal had been served, she realized the dishwasher was broken. So she washed the dinner dishes by hand. It was nearly ten o'clock when she arrived home.

When she checked her messages, she found two from Jefferson. She erased both of his messages shortly after his hello, took a shower, got a book, and climbed into bed. The phone rang, startling her. She reached over and took it off the hook without putting it to her ear. She didn't want to talk to anyone.

***

"So? You want to talk or do you just want to sit in a silent funk? And if it's the latter, why the hell did you call me over here?"

Jefferson took a deep breath before he exploded from his favorite easy chair to his feet. He paced the length of his rec room, trying in vain to control his emotions.

106

He turned to stare at Ben, who sprawled in a matching padded leather recliner a few feet from the one he'd just vacated. Dressed in dark sweats, with his gaze trained on the large plasma TV along on wall, Ben appeared disinterested. Jefferson knew him well enough to know better.

He strolled over to the terrace doors. "How the hell am I ever going to convince her I didn't sleep with that woman? She is never going to believe me. She's going to blame me for something that never happened!"

"Maybe it's for the best."

He swung around to face Ben. "What? How the hell can it be for the best for her to think I slept with another woman the same night I made love to her?"

"Well, you were looking for a way out of the mess sleeping with her landed you in and now you have it."

"What mess? What the fucking hell are you ranting about, Ben? My life is falling apart around me and you're getting delusional on me? What the fuck makes you think sleeping with her was a mistake?"

"You know my motto, Jeff, don't mix business with pleasure. How can sleeping with your second in command, for whom you have no real feelings, be anything but a mistake?"

"No real feelings? What the hell have you been smoking? You know damn well I care about her."

Ben shrugged. "Let's call it like it is. You two were alone, you were both feeling horny, and you surrendered to your lust. Then, womanlike, instead of recognizing you just needed no-strings-attached sex, she wants to go and imagine you give a fuck about her or her feelings on an emotional level."

"What the fuck! I do care about her feelings! How the hell can you think this is just about sex? It was sex with Vanessa..."

"And with Sharde? If it wasn't just sex, why didn't you offer her the reassurance she so clearly needed and wanted from you, Jeff? Why offer the lovely but worthless Vanessa marriage after one weekend and then tell Sharde she's unreasonable to expect you to do the same with her?"

He stared at Ben. "Are you implying that I...what the hell are you implying?"

"I'm implying that it's time you woke up and realized Sharde is the real deal and act accordingly. Linda and Vanessa were both harpies who were more interested in your cock size and your financial bottom line. Sharde, strange soul that she is, seems to actually care about your big ugly ass. I honestly think if you were a clerk in some corporate mailroom, she'd still be in love with you. We both know the same could not be said for either Linda or Vanessa.

"If you don't want to lose Sharde, tell her what she needs to hear. If she wants a commitment, give her one."

"She wants to get married and have kids."

"And you don't want either one of those things?"

"You know damn well I want them both."

"Just not with her?"

"I...I do want them...with her."

"Then why the hell did you pick up Sally Bimbo last night?"

"It was a mistake, but I swear, nothing happened, Ben."

He shrugged. "I believe you, but I'm not the one you have to convince. If I were you, I'd go buy several pairs of pads for your knees because you are going to be begging big time. Then, if you're lucky, she'll either believe you or not believe you, but decide to forgive you anyway."

"For something I haven't done?"

Ben laughed. "Don't get self-righteous, Jeff. You did take

her home…that's going to be an awful big hurdle for you to overcome."

He raked a hand through his hair. "You know she won't talk to me."

"She's hurt. Give her another day or so."

"It was her idea."

"Jeff, it's time you grew up and admit you don't know jack about women."

"And you know about women?"

Ben grinned. "Hey, I'm not the one in deep shit with the only woman I care about."

He swallowed slowly. "I do care about her, Ben…more than I thought possible."

"I know that."

"So where did I go wrong?"

"If a woman you've just done tells you to go see other women *after* you've refused to give her the big C, do not be gullible enough to believe she means it.

"Give her another day or so and then pour your heart out to her and beg for mercy. It doesn't matter that you didn't actually do the other woman. The fact that you took her home is going to matter."

"Damn, Ben, I'm screwed!"

Ben arched a brow. "Big time."

***

Sharde slept badly Saturday night, woke late on Sunday morning, showered, had two boiled eggs and a cup of coffee, and spent the rest of the day at the shelter.

She arrived home just after six to find Jeff had called twice. She erased his messages, hesitated, and then took her phone off the hook. Undressing, she took a long bubble bath. Around nine-thirty when she finally wrapped a towel around her body and made her way to her bedroom, the front door buzzer sounded.

She walked over to the console and looked at her video caller ID. Jefferson stood in the lobby in front of the camera, holding a bouquet of flowers. If he thought flowers would make up for his having slept with another woman the first time they had an argument, he was nuts.

Ignoring the ache in her chest, she left him standing there and went back into the bathroom. She closed the door and turned on the radio. She had eaten her heart out for Jefferson Calder for the last time.

She found another message waiting when she emerged from the bathroom an hour later.

She pushed the playback button. "Sharde, I know you're upset, but we need to talk. Please pick up. Just talk to me. Please. After we talk, if you want me to go, I will, but please just give me a chance to explain."

She erased the message, tossed a salad, turned off her ringer, and went to bed.

***

On Monday morning, Jefferson arrived at work and found his world had crashed down around him. He had felt bad when he lost the defense contract after months of long hours and hard work. His heart had ached when first Linda and then Vanessa cheated on him. As he stared at Sharde's resignation lying on the center of his desk, he felt sick and afraid.

He raked his hands through his hair, panic and desperation eating at him. He couldn't seem to catch his breath. This could not be happening. He should not feel as if his heart was being ripped out of his body. For that to happen he would have to love her. And he didn't.

He felt an undeniable need to be with her. He wanted her more than he'd ever wanted another woman. The sex between them was explosive and consuming. And he was even finally ready to propose if she'd only give him a chance to atone for his dumb mistake. He cared deeply about her…enough to risk marriage again. But he did not love her.

No? Then why the hell do you feel as if your heart is not only breaking, but also cracking into pieces so tiny you'll never be able to recover or love another woman?

He had tried to apologize but she was determined not to forgive him. What the hell was he supposed to do if she wouldn't talk to him or see him? He stiffened. She had the power to refuse to see him outside of work, but not here.

He rose and stalked down the long corridor separating their offices, knocked on her door, waited a second, opened the door, and entered.

She sat at her desk, pouring over what he recognized as application folders. She didn't look up. "Look, I'm busy right now. I need to get these employment applications done. Come back this afternoon, please."

He closed the door and leaned against it. "They can wait. We need to talk."

She stiffened and looked up at him, a weary look in her eyes. "There's nothing to talk about, Jefferson. I gave you your options, you made your choice, and now it's time for both of us to move on."

He sighed and spread his hands wide, feeling helpless. "I know you called my house and I know a woman answered, but nothing happened between us, Sharde. Nothing."

"Oh. I see. You took her home for companionship."

"I was hurt, angry, and horny. I took her home to fuck her," he said bluntly. "But I didn't…" He sighed. "I…couldn't."

She shook her head. "You know what, Jefferson? It doesn't matter. I don't care. I want more from a relationship than you want to give. It's time for me to move on and find a man who's not afraid to entrust his heart to me."

"You want a proposal? Fine. Marry me."

She shook her head again. "If you had offered that meaningless proposal last week, I would have said yes. But I finally have my priorities straight. I want you sexually, but I don't need you anymore." She lifted her chin. "So please just let it go, Jefferson."

He swallowed rapidly, several times. He closed his eyes briefly, an ache inside him that threatened to overwhelm him. "I did not sleep with her. I swear I didn't."

"All that matters is that you took her home to sleep with her! It doesn't matter why or even if you did. We have one argument and you immediately go pick up some long-legged blonde and spend the night with her."

"She wasn't a blonde, but you don't care, do you? Because you are hell-bent on being a self-righteous, unforgiving bitch, aren't you? Never mind you were the one who goaded me into the whole damn mess in the first place! You know damn well when we went to your place another woman was the last thing on my mind."

Her lips trembled and her eyes shot angry sparks at him. "You betray me and then have the nerve to call me a bitch? And don't you dare try to blame me! I didn't go pick up a man and take him home with me." She snatched up the application folders and tossed them at him. "Leave me alone!"

He tilted his head to one side to avoid the folders.

She bolted to her feet and rushed across the room to hit her fists against his shoulders. "I spent nine long, miserable years wanting you! Nine years, Jeff. I stood by and watched you eat your heart out for Linda and then Vanessa. Finally I get my turn. We have one argument and the first thing you do is take another woman to bed!"

He allowed her to hit him, only turning his head slightly when she came too close to his face. "I did not sleep with her." He cupped his hands around her face and stared down at her. "I swear I didn't."

"But you took her home. What happened? Were you too drunk to perform?"

He flushed. "I don't get that drunk."

She jerked away from him, bent, and began picking up the application folders. When he stooped to help her, she slapped his hand away. "Just please get out and leave me alone, Jefferson. You've finally cured me of my addiction to you. I don't want or need anything from you. I am willing to stay for a few weeks until new system analysts are hired, and then I'm leaving. Darbi is quite capable of handling all my responsibilities."

"I didn't come here to discuss Darbi."

"I don't give a flying fuck why you came here! If you don't leave me alone, I will walk out right now and not look back."

"You think I care about anything right now except making things right with you?"

"You can't make them right! I've finally seen the light. You were never worth my time or the numerous heartaches I suffered on your behalf. There is nothing you can say or do to make me change my mind. Just leave me alone. Please, Jeff."

He sucked in a deep breath. His knees shook and his chest ached. His heart shattered. Standing there looking down into her hostile gaze, he knew his foolish mistake had cost him a woman he had loved without even knowing it.

"I'm so sorry. I...I never meant to hurt you."

"You did, but it's the best thing you could have done for

me because I am finally free of my need and desire for you." She hit a fist against his shoulder. "Please, Jefferson. Just leave me alone."

He heard pain in her voice, saw anguish in her eyes. Fighting back the desire to sweep her up into his arms and hold her until she stopped hurting, he turned and left the office.

He heard what sounded like a sob but kept walking. She was not in the mood to consider forgiveness or to hear anything he had to say. She certainly didn't want to accept comfort from him. He had hurt her. She would need time to heal and rage at him.

He would wait and bide his time. He wasn't going to let her slip through his fingers without one hell of a fight.

CHAPTER EIGHT

Four weeks later, Sharde received a call that both surprised and intrigued her. Two nights later, she had dinner at an exclusive restaurant with Clayton Frazier of Fra-Tech, Inc. He wore a tailor-made suit that complimented his athletic six-foot-six frame and highlighted his piercing sea-green eyes. Dark hair, silvering at the temples, contrasted nicely with skin tanned a mouth-watering honey bronze by the tropical sun. He nearly took her breath away.

He must spend a lot of time in the tropics where she'd heard both his parents lived. If she weren't so in love with Jeff, just looking at Clayton Frazier would send her lust meter off the scale.

As it was, it was difficult not to lick her lips every time she looked into those amazing eyes. Now that she'd met him, she could understand how Vanessa had rapidly fallen into lust with him. There was something so completely sensual and sexy about the man, she couldn't imagine any woman not wanting to drop her drawers and engage in hot monkey sex, given the least sign of encouragement from him.

Not that she was under any illusions as to why he'd asked her out to dinner. Although it was flattering to be wined and dined by a man so handsome other women gaped in obvious envy, it was time she made her position clear.

"Mr. Frazier—"

"Clay or Clayton, please."

His warm, deep voice, combined with his stunning good

MARILYN LEE

looks, sent a chill of pure, unadulterated lust through her every time he spoke. It didn't matter what he said or how he said it. Holy hell, but the man was sexiness personified.

She resisted the urge to moisten her lips. "Clayton, this has been a lovely evening, but the answer is still no."

A small smile pulled at the corners of his full-lipped mouth. "Even if I promise that if you come to work for Fra-Tech I would never want or expect you to divulge any information detrimental to Calder? I know your relationship went beyond business and I would—"

She caught her breath and leaned forward. "What? What makes you think that?"

His gaze swept over her face. "How could he possibly resist getting to know you better after working with you for so long?"

"What do you mean?"

"I mean he's a normal man and you're an attractive woman and you're both unattached."

Gazing into his eyes, she saw no evidence of guile. Hot damn, the hottest hunk she'd ever met thought she was attractive. But then, judging by the hunger she'd felt when Jeff made love to her, Jeff had thought so as well. "My relationship with Mr. Calder has no bearing on my decision to decline your offer to work at Fra-Tech, Clayton."

"I see." He sipped his coffee. "If you should change your mind, there will always be a place for you at Fra-Tech."

She smiled, warmed by his sincerity. "Thank you."

"Now that we have business out of the way, let's get personal."

Her heart raced. "In what way?"

"Judging by the furious look on Calder's face, I'm assuming you're no longer seeing him, so—"

"I was never seeing him."

He arched a brow. "Weren't you?"

"No!" You could hardly call what they'd shared dating. She blinked at him. "On his face? What do you mean? When did you see him?"

"Now." His gaze narrowed. "He's sitting across the room. If you look over your right shoulder, you'll see him glaring in this direction."

A wave of heat rushed up her neck and into her face as she half turned. Several tables away Jeff sat at a table, facing her back. A broad-shouldered man with short, honey-blond hair she recognized as Ben shared Jeff's table.

She met the cold, accusing look in Jeff's eyes briefly before turning to face Clayton again. The desire to rush over to Jeff's table and assure him that she would never do or say anything to hurt Calder Technologies financially was difficult to overcome. But if he didn't know that without being told, a thousand assurances from her wouldn't make any difference.

"That's the face of a jealous lover if ever I've seen one, and I've seen more than my share."

With looks and charisma like his, she was certain he had. She shrugged. "He has no reason to be jealous."

He arched a brow. "Why so sure? I didn't ask you out entirely for business reasons."

She swallowed quickly. "You didn't?"

"Not entirely, no. Now that business has been dealt with let's get personal. I'd like to see you again in a strictly social setting."

She looked in his eyes and was almost tempted. If anyone could help her shake her hunger for Jeff, Clayton certainly could. The thought of lying in bed with him, having him fuck her senseless, nearly made her melt. But no matter how sexually appealing she found him, he was the man for whom Vanessa had left Jeff. For her to start even a strictly sexual relationship with him after rejecting Jeff's efforts to reconcile would be extremely painful for Jeff.

And despite her best efforts, she was still too much in love with him to want to deliver such a blow to his ego. "That's a tempting proposition, Clayton, but—"

"Excuse the interruption, but this is a surprise, Sharde."

She glanced up. Ben, a question in his gaze, his voice cool, paused at their table. Jeff stalked past the table without glancing their way.

"Ben. Long time no see." She forced a smile and glanced at Clayton, who seemed completely at ease. "Clayton, this is Benton Savage. Ben, this is Clayton Frazier."

Clayton rose with a smile. She watched as he and Ben shook hands.

Ben looked at Clayton. "Would it be too much trouble to ask to speak to Sharde alone for a few moments?"

Clayton's smiled vanished. "I don't usually go off and leave my date alone with other men."

"I can sympathize, but Sharde and I are old friends."

Clayton turned to study her face. "Sharde?"

Although she had no desire to be left alone with Ben, the look in his gaze hinted that he was determined. She glanced at Clayton and noted a similar determination to ensure nothing happened she didn't want. Knowing Ben was not above making a scene on Jefferson's behalf, she nodded. "Would you excuse us for a few moments, Clayton?"

"You're sure?"

She was sure there would be a scene if she didn't. And she was not in the mood for that. "Yes, I'm sure."

He looked at Ben. "Remember she's my date and don't take too much of her time." He spoke in a cold tone.

Ben's lips tightened. Fearful he would precipitate a scene by telling Clayton to go the hell, Sharde placed a hand on his arm and squeezed.

He gave Clayton a curt nod. "Understood."

Clayton smiled at her and walked away from the table.

Ben sat down and took her clenched fist between his palms. "What the hell are you doing with the competition, Sharde? Seeing you with Frazier has knocked the starch out of Jeff."

She jerked at her hand. "What I'm not doing is divulging any Calder Technologies secrets!"

Ben tightened his grip. "That's not what I meant since that goes without saying. I mean what are you doing with the same man Vanessa left him for? The same man who outbid him on one of the company's biggest deals? Seeing you with him stings Jeff on a very personal level, honey."

"Don't honey me, Ben, and he gave up the right to care who I see when he made his lack of feelings for me clear."

He shook his head. "You know damn well that's not true, Sharde. Or you should…you would…if you weren't so blinded by the desire to hurt him emotionally. Hanging out with Frazier is so beneath you."

His accusatory tone stung. She jerked at her hand again. "Don't you preach to me, Ben! I wasted nine years on his butt and I'll be damned if I'll waste another second waiting on him. He didn't want to commit and I wasn't interested in being his booty call."

"Now we both know he didn't treat you like any booty call!" He grinned. "Although I will admit that you do have a rather luscious ass. I've occasionally been tempted."

She blushed. "Ben!"

"What? I'm supposed to be blind because you're my best friend's woman?"

"I'm not his woman."

"The hell you're not!" He glanced over his shoulder and sighed. "Your watchdog Frazier is glaring in this direction so I guess we'll have to have this conversation at another time."

She shook her head. "There's nothing to talk about."

He released her hand and rose. "Oh, yes there is. Sharde?"

When she glanced up, he leaned down and pressed a light kiss against her lips. "Put me out of my misery and forgive him. Please, or I swear all his whining will drive me to drink again!"

She pushed at his shoulder. "Stay out of this, Ben!"

"Not damned likely." He kissed her lips again and walked away.

Face burning, she watched Clayton return to their table, his brow arched. "A friend, did you say?"

"Yes...and before you ask, without benefits. We usually do the cheek thing when we meet."

"So why kiss you twice tonight?"

She shrugged. "I think he only kissed me to annoy you."

Clayton laughed and resumed his seat. "Mission accomplished. It annoyed the hell out of me to see my date being kissed by another man."

"That's the first time he's ever kissed me on the lips!"

"Really? Well. Since this is a night for firsts..." He rose and moved to stand by her chair. When she looked up at him, he bent and pressed a long, hot kiss against her lips that made her pussy gush.

She pushed against his shoulder and he finally lifted his head and resumed his seat.

"Why did you do that?"

"I've been wanting to do it all night."

"Ahhh…it's getting late. I think—"

"It's early yet. Would you like to go dancing?"

If she danced with him no power on earth would be strong enough to keep her out of his bed if he wanted her there. And she was not about to sleep with him. She smiled. "That's a tempting offer, but I think I'd better go home."

"In love with him, huh?"

"No. I told you Ben and I are just friends."

"I didn't mean Savage. I meant Calder."

"Yes," she whispered, afraid that if she didn't, Clayton might press her. And no matter how much her body ached to sleep with him, she couldn't betray Jeff in that way. "So when you take me home, please don't call me again."

"I'll take you home, but as for not calling you again?" He shrugged. "I'll think about it. If he's foolish enough not to stake a claim on you, he'll have to risk losing you."

"You can have any woman you want."

"Maybe I want you."

"When you could have had Vanessa?"

"I didn't want Del Warren."

"She's gorgeous."

He shrugged. "I'm sure many men would agree with that assessment of her…charms, but I'm not one of them. I no longer judge a woman strictly on physical appearances. I'm old enough to find other qualities equally as important. And in addition to her obvious lack of fidelity, she's not my type."

"And I am?"

"You're attractive, intelligent, loyal, and you have the right skin tone. Why wouldn't you be my type?"

"Men like you are usually interested in a beautiful trophy wife."

"Are they?" He shrugged. "Maybe so."

"Then?"

"My father's family was from the old South where gentle-men did not prefer blondes. I come from a long line of Frazier men who embrace that old southern tradition."

"Oh." She frowned, eyeing him. "But isn't your mother..."

"White? Yes. Don't let this deep tan fool you. I spend a lot of time in the islands, where I was born." A smile curved his lips. "Mom's a beautiful blonde trophy, all right. But like my father, her taste runs to lovers with darker skin tones."

"Oh." She blinked. "Both of them?"

He laughed at the dismay she couldn't keep out of her voice. "Yes, both of them. They are both in long-term relationships with their island lovers and I have two younger biracial siblings to prove it...one from each parent."

She parted her lips.

He shook his head. "If you say oh again, I'll be forced to kiss you into saying something else."

She blushed, and then laughed.

He smiled. "That's better." He tilted his head. "Are you sure you won't come dancing with me?"

She sighed. "I would love to go dancing with you, but I don't dare."

He reached across the table to touch her hand. "You don't need to be afraid of me, honey. Nothing will happen between us that you don't want."

Normally, having a man call her honey on a first date would annoy her. But the endearment, spoken in that low, deep voice of his with just the hint of a southern drawl conjured up lust-ful thoughts of long nights of endless fucking—of both her entrances. First date? That assumed there would be other dates. She swallowed slowly. "That's what I'm afraid of—wanting something to happen."

"Why?"

"I can't do that to him. Not with you...not after Vanessa."

"Look, let's clear the air. I didn't want nor did I chase his woman."

"You took her from him."

"The hell I did! I told you she is not my type. She came to me and offered to get information to help me outbid him."

"What?!"

He shook his head. "Wait a minute. Don't get the wrong idea. She offered, but I did not accept. I told her to take her faithless ass out of my office and never spoke to her again."

She stared at him.

He stared back. "We won that bid fair and square, Sharde. In business, I'm not going to make any apologies for not taking any prisoners, but I do not cheat. We earned that contract fair and square. I hope you believe that."

"I don't know why I should, but I do."

He smiled. "I'm glad to hear it. As for her, if he can't see she did him a favor by walking out on him, he's dumber than I thought."

"He's very intelligent."

"Then how do you explain his falling for her or his allowing you get away from him? Such asinine behavior qualifies as dumb in my book."

"Love is blind."

"Maybe so, but does it have to be dumb as well?"

She stared at him and then laughed. As she did, she felt much of the tension she'd been feeling for so long ease. She sat back in her seat. "You are certainly good for a woman's ego."

"I wouldn't have thought your ego needed any help."

It did when she loved a man who didn't love her. "I think I'm going to like you far more than I should."

"I have that effect on intelligent, discriminating women." He grinned at her. "So. Come dancing with me? Before you say no I promise I won't grind against you and at the end of the night I will take you home and leave you there alone. No pressure. I just want to dance with you. So what do you say?"

***

"Do you want to talk about it. . .her. . .them?"

Jefferson paced the length of his rec room, raking his hands through his hair. A knot of rage tightened in his gut as he briefly thought of Sharde with Frazier. The two of them might even now be in bed together. She might be allowing Frazier to do things to and with her that she had not allowed him to do.

"I should have punched his damned lights out!"

"So you want to talk about him?"

He swung around and stared at Ben, who sprawled in one of the two chairs in front of the plasma TV. "No. If I talk about it. . .I swear I'll wring his damned neck. . .if he touches her. . ."

"It will be because it's what she wants."

He swallowed hard to dislodge the lump in his throat. He shook his head. "She won't sleep with him."

"You sound very sure of that."

"I am. She may be angry with me but we've been friends almost since the moment we met. She wouldn't do that to me. I know she wouldn't."

"Even if she thought you'd betrayed her with Sally Bimbo?"

"Even then."

"Okay. So you know she won't betray any company secrets

and you know she won't sleep with him. Why are you so upset?"

"Because she's my woman and she has no damn business seeing him or anyone else!" He walked over to his chair and sank down into it. "I miss her. Damn, I've been a fool. I thought I wasn't ready for commitment with her because I told her it was just physical between us...I mean I knew I cared about her on a personal level..."

"So what are you going to do?"

"Win her back."

"Ready to do what you need to do?"

"It's not that simple. She—"

Ben bolted to his feet. "Look, Jeff, if you're not going to lose her, you'd better get your ass with the program. I'm thinking Frazier would love to snatch her right out of your grasp. If that's what you want to happen, keep thinking you have time to play games."

He sighed. "I know, but I don't think she's ready to even talk to me, let alone forgive me."

He shrugged. "You could be right. Just don't wait too long...or she may do something with Frazier you'll both regret."

"If he touches her, I swear, I'll—"

"Don't give him the chance. Take care of business."

CHAPTER NINE

Two days later, Sharde met Darbi for lunch at the mall near All Faiths. Picking at her salad, she told Darbi of her date with Clayton Frazier.

"So he's...what was he like?"

She shook her head. "He is the most gorgeous hunk I've ever seen. Oh, lord, Darbi when he kissed me, I swear I nearly had a heart attack. He reeks of sex appeal. You look in his eyes and you just want to rip off your clothes and let him fuck you until your pussy is dry and numb and then you'd let him do it all over again."

"So why did you refuse to see him again?"

"I couldn't do that to Jeff."

"Still in love with him?"

"Yes. Clayton is hot, but my feelings for Jeff go beyond the physical." She sighed. "How is he?"

"Miserable. You know he broke down and asked me about you."

"And you told him?"

Darbi shrugged. "I wanted to tell him I wasn't going to discuss you, but he looked so hungry for information, I told him you were fine. So how are you?"

"In the last few days, I've been kissed by two of the most attractive men in the city." Recalling her date with Clayton, she smiled. "Of course I'm fine."

"You have a far away look in your eyes. What are you thinking of?"

MARILYN LEE

"Dancing with Clayton," she admitted. "Oh, Darbi, girl, it ought to be against the law for any one man to be so damned sexy. While we danced all I could think of was hot monkey sex. One minute we were slow dancing and I was longing for Jeff, the next, I looked in Clayton's eyes and I was sooo tempted to spend the night with him."

"To get back at Jefferson?"

"No! For the pleasure of having him fuck me! I'm telling you, Darbi, he is hot."

"So you've replaced fantasies of Jefferson with those of Frazier?"

"No!" Her cheeks burned. "I know it might sound like that, but no. My attraction to Clayton was powerful, but strictly physical. I'm in love with Jefferson *and* sexually attracted to him."

"I'm glad to hear that because I don't think he could recover if you had an affair with Frazier."

She frowned. "I'm not having an affair with him! We had one date. Period. At the end of the night, he went home..." She grinned. "After kissing me until my toes curled. I think there was actually smoke pouring out the top of my head."

Darbi tilted her head. "If you're not going to end up in Frazier's bed, I'm thinking you'd better forgive Jefferson pronto and put you both out of your misery."

She shook her head. "I want to, but I can't allow myself to be hurt anymore. I need more than he's willing to give me."

"Are you sure that's still true? He's been so miserable since you left, he might have had time to change his mind."

"Maybe." She moistened her lips. "Now that you're working so closely with him...how do you two get along?"

Darbi smiled. "Strictly like a boss and an employee. We don't do lunch and we have no shared outside interests. And we haven't shared a single smooch. I haven't spent a single Sunday watching a ball game with him and I don't plan to—not that he'd want me to. Don't worry, Sharde, we have zero personal interest in each other."

She laughed, shaking her head. "I'm sorry. I shouldn't even have asked that. It's just that...you're so beautiful and he's so handsome and horny."

"Maybe so, but he's not horny for me. And I'm not interested in him."

"Why not?"

She shrugged. "Granted, he is handsome and he can be charming, but he just doesn't do anything for me. And I am very sure I don't do anything for him. He doesn't look like the kind of man who could appreciate a full-figured woman."

Sharde grimaced. "I'm not exactly a size six."

"No, but you're not full-figured either. But I'm thinking he's really missing you. Why don't you give him a call and see if you can work things out?"

"He's the one who strayed after our first fight. If he wants me enough, he's going to have to be willing to crawl a little."

"And if he's not?"

She sighed. "Then things will stay as they are and I'll continue without him. It's not the way I want it, but I can do it, if I have to."

"And Frazier? Would you date him?"

"I don't know." She tilted her head. "If not for the past hostility between he and Jeff, I'd definitely go out with him."

"If you're not going to end up in bed with Frazier, I think you'd better not see him again."

"I'm not going to sleep with him!"

"You wouldn't sound so certain if you could see your face when you're talking about how hot he is."

"He is hot, but that doesn't mean I'm going to bed with him. What about you? I know things have been difficult since the divorce and the failed relationships, but you deserve to be happy too."

"I know and I will…but right now I just want to concentrate on me without the complication of a man in my life."

Sharde sighed. That Martin and the two jerks that followed him had a lot to answer for. "You know who would rock your world big time?"

"Who?"

"Clayton."

"As in Frazier?"

"Yes."

"What makes you think he'd be interested in giving me what I need?"

She shrugged. "I don't know. I just know the two of you would make one beautiful couple. You're gorgeous and he's beyond handsome. And Darbi, he likes black women."

"Does he?"

She nodded. "He said it's an old southern tradition he's been following since high school."

"So he likes black women for what? For sex or for marriage?"

"I don't know." She frowned. After all, both his parents preferred black lovers, but were still married to each other. "I'll ask him."

"You're seeing him again?"

"He said he'd ask me again and he's very persistent. It's not easy to say no to him."

"If you're not going to end up in bed with him, you'd better steer clear of him. But his preference in a woman he wants to marry doesn't really matter anyway. I'm fine for now. Granted

I'm a little horny, but I'll be all right. You're the one I'm worried about."

"Don't. I'll be all right too—with or without Jefferson."

A week later Sharde met Clayton at her favorite seafood restaurant. They discussed movies, sports, and politics; she found herself liking him even more. When he asked her to have dinner with him two nights later, she reluctantly refused.

"Look, honey, I know you're in love with Calder and I'm not looking to get in your bed," he told her, as they stood by her car in the parking lot.

"Aren't you? Why else would you be pursuing me?"

He frowned. "Look, at the risk of sounding vain, I'll tell you that I have never met a woman I wanted that I didn't get. Never. If I wanted you in my bed, you'd end up there sooner or later."

Although she shook her head, she suspected he was right. "So you don't want me in your bed. Charming, Clayton."

He laughed and shook his head. "That came out all wrong. Let me rephrase that. If I was hell-bent on going to bed with you and that was my primary interest in you, you'd end up in my bed."

"Then what are you looking for? What do you want from me?"

"Don't misunderstand, honey. If you weren't so in love with bonehead, I'd be delighted to make love to you, but I've accepted the limitations you've placed on our relationship." He shrugged. "Can't we just be friends?"

"Jefferson wouldn't like—"

"Really? Does he choose your friends for you?"

She shook her head. "I can't believe I was about to say that. Of course, he doesn't choose my friends."

"Good. Because sometimes I just want feminine company

without…" He paused. "After my other remark this is really going to sound vain beyond words, but, hell, that's how it is. I get tired of women coming onto me. Sometimes I just want to be with a woman without any sexual connotation." He grinned. "Granted that doesn't happen often, but when it does , may I call you?"

She stared up at him, surprised at how at ease she felt with him. "I do like you."

"I like you. So. And anytime you want to do something about our mutual like, I'd be happy to oblige."

She sighed. "Please don't tempt me."

He laughed. "Until then we'll be friends." He extended his hand. "Shake on it?"

When she placed her hand in his, he bent his head and brushed his lips against her cheek. "And if you need a male perspective or want someone to give Calder a kick in his dumb ass to get him moving in the right direction, I'll be at your disposal, honey."

She laughed and got in her car. "You keep your big feet on the ground. I like his ass just as it is."

He closed her car door. "I'll give you a little space and then I'll call you. Okay?"

She nodded. "Okay."

When he bent to kiss her cheek, she turned her head and his lips brushed lightly against hers.

She caught her breath and then parted her lips.

He pressed a long, warm kiss against her mouth before nibbling at her lips. "Anytime you want to change the rules…" He cupped his palm around the back of her head and licked her lips. A tingle of desire danced down her spine. "We can be friends—with benefits," he murmured. "Lots of benefits…benefits we can share as often as you like."

Friends with benefits. She couldn't accept that from Jefferson because she was in love with him. She needed more than that from him. But why shouldn't she try it with Clayton? If she couldn't get what her heart needed from Jefferson, why shouldn't she allow her body the sweet release she was certain she could find in Clayton's bed?

Why should she care how Jefferson would feel if he learned she and Clayton were lovers? Because she loved him. She shook her head and drew away from him. "I would really like that."

"So would I. So why don't we do it?"

"You know why."

"If he doesn't come up to scratch soon, I just might decide he's not worthy of you."

"Then what?"

"Then I'd go into pursuit mode and you *would* end up in my bed." He touched her cheek. "And once I had you there, I'm thinking I wouldn't be inclined to let you go—ever."

She stared at him. "What are you saying?"

He kissed her cheek and straightened. "Good night, honey."

"Clayton? You didn't answer my question."

"I don't think you really want me to answer it. Just know that if he doesn't want you in a way you want him to, there are other men who do and will."

"I don't understand."

He stroked her cheek. "Oh, I think you do."

"We've only seen each other a couple of times and—"

"I've been interested in you since I saw you at a trade show three years ago."

"What?"

"But it was clear even then that you only had eyes for him. Not that that would have stopped me."

"You're very sure of yourself, aren't you?"

"Women have given me reason to be."

That she could well believe. "So what did stop you?"

"I didn't want you to think I was asking you out in an attempt to get Calder Tech secrets. But once I learned you'd left the company...I called you. And here we are."

She stared up at him. How could this gorgeous hunk have wanted to date her for three years while she'd been eating her heart out for Jefferson? If she had known of his interest then... "I...I should go."

"Yes, you should...before I decide to come with you. If that happens, we'll end up spending the night together."

"You said you only wanted to be friends."

"What I want right now is you in bed."

She moistened her lips.

"You don't want that. Do you, honey?"

She swallowed the *yes* trembling on her lips. "Good night." She closed her driver's side window, secured her seatbelt, and drove away.

After a long soak, while she tried not to think of what Clayton had said, meant, or implied, she fell asleep...

Naked, she ran along a moonlight beach. Clayton, naked and aroused, chased her. As she glanced over her shoulder to gauge how close he was, she fell. Before she could scramble to her feet, he was on the sand beside her, rolling her on to her back, mounting her, and pushing his hard legs between her thighs. She cried out in an agony of pleasure as he drove his cock balls deep into her with a thrust so powerful, her toes curled and her back arched.

"I knew you wanted to be friends with benefits, you sweet honey. Now I have you and you are mine and this is my pussy!" He groaned as he slid his hands under her ass and fucked her wet pussy with long, deep, hard strokes that drove her wild with lust. Each time he drew partway out of her, she sobbed in

protest, tightening herself around him. And when he drove his powerful hips down, and his hot cock plowed back into her, she shuddered and clung to him.

"Oh, Clay. . .don't ever stop."

Unwilling to part with even an inch of his wonderful dick, she wrapped her legs around him and fucked herself on his cock until she came and came.

Then he shot his seed into her, withdrew, turned her onto her stomach, spread her legs, and slid his big body over hers. She closed her eyes and clenched her hands into fists at her side as she felt his cock slipping between her cheeks.

"No," she whispered. "No, Clay, no. Take as much pussy as you like, but this belongs only to Jeff."

"Bonehead had his chance and blew it. Now, you and this beautiful ass of yours belong to me, honey," he whispered and pressed his dick against her puckered opening. "And I'm going to fuck you there to prove it."

Instead of resisting, as she knew she should, she moaned and lifted her hips, eager to feel the first inch of his hard cock taking possession of her ass.

He gripped her hips and she moaned with pleasure as the big head of his cock pushed its way past her protesting opening, and halfway up her rectum. "Oh, no!"

"Oh, yes! Feels good, doesn't it, honey?"

"Yes," she whispered in a small, shamed voice. "Oh, Clay, yes!"

"It's getting ready to feel even better." Settling his weight on her, he slipped his hands under her body to cup her breasts, bit the side of her neck, and slowly forced the rest of his cock in her until he was buried to the hilt in her ass.

"Oh, honey, I knew your ass would be as tight and sweet as your pussy." He slowly fucked his cock in and out of her ass, sending waves of lust crashing over her. She moaned and luxuriated in every wonderful hot stroke as he bottomed out in her over and over. With each stroke, he lay a claim to her that she was too weak to challenge.

He leaned over her and rained biting kisses on her neck and shoulders as he fucked her with deep, painful strokes until she sobbed his name and came. "Clayton! Clayton! Oh, Clayton, don't ever stop fucking me!"

Sharde bolted into a sitting position in her darkened bedroom, her heart pounding. It took her several moments to realize that she'd been dreaming. Dreaming? She fell back against her bed. Dreaming that Jeff had anal sex with her was dreaming. Doing the same with Clayton was a nightmare.

Darbi had been right. She shouldn't see Clayton again. If she did, they were definitely going to end up as lovers, with her joyfully welcoming him into all her openings, pussy, ass, and mouth. She shuddered at the thought of Clayton's cock sliding into her. Although she had never actually seen his cock, she had felt it a few times as they slow danced. From what she had felt she knew he had nothing to be ashamed of, size-wise.

"Stop it, Sharde!" She turned and buried her burning face against her pillow.

When Clayton called and asked her to have dinner with him a week later, she told him she needed some time to deal with issues before they saw each other again.

"Damn, honey. Are you sure? I'm going to visit my parents and will be out of the country for several weeks. I don't suppose you'd like to come with me?"

"I can't, Clay."

"Damn. Okay." He sighed. "I'll call you."

"Okay. Have a safe trip."

"I'd enjoy it more if you came with me."

"I can't, Clay."

A dozen roses sat outside her condo door that evening.

I'm going to miss you, honey. Miss me too. Clay.

"I will, Clay," she said softly.

Later that night, she dreamed of Clayton and Jefferson both begging her to marry them. She woke the next morning with the memory of having chosen Clayton—after he spent a night making love to her in every conceivable way. When he called her a week later, they talked for over an hour.

As she listened to his deep, warm voice, she imagined him whispering all kinds of naughty things in her ear and got aroused.

"I think you should know that when I return, I'll be in full pursuit mode and to hell with bonehead," he told her.

She sighed. She'd wasted nine years and a number of weeks waiting for Jefferson. Maybe it was time to count her emotional losses and start fresh—with Clayton. He certainly seemed to want her. "Clay, I—"

"You don't need to say anything, honey. I know how you feel about bonehead…and how I feel about you. I'm tired of playing nice. Since I promised you nothing you didn't want to happen would ever happen between us, I wanted to give you a heads up. When I return, no more Mr. Nice Guy. My goal is going to be to land you in my bed."

"I wish you wouldn't talk like that."

"Why not?"

"It makes me hot," she admitted.

"And when you get hot does your pussy get wet and your nipples harden? Do you want to know what's hard on me?"

She took several deep breaths. "You're only making me hotter!"

He laughed. "That's the idea. Damn, I wish I hadn't promised my mother I'd spend a few weeks with her." He sighed. "I'd better go before I get too aroused."

"Clay…"

"Yes?"

She bit back the urge to tell him she'd be waiting when he returned. "I…"

"You can tell me when we see each other in a couple of weeks."

"A couple of week seems a long time."

"A very long time. Are you ready to give us a try?"

Jeff would find her sleeping with Clay unforgivable. If she took that final step any lingering hope she had of resuming a relationship with Jeff would be destroyed. Her body was ready for that step, but was her heart?

"Never mind. You can tell me when we see each other again. Good night, sweetheart."

"Good night, Clay."

It took several hours for her to fall asleep that night. As she dressed the next morning, a dozen roses were delivered.

I can't wait to see you again, honey. Clay.

She sighed. She would face the biggest decision of her life when he returned.

Four weeks later, tired from a ten-hour day at the shelter and confused by her mounting lust for Clayton while still in love with Jefferson, Sharde walked to her car. She had been putting in long days since she'd started. Dianne had insisted she not return until Wednesday.

The long days at the shelter were tiring but rewarding. Her severance package from Calder Technologies had been more generous than she'd expected. She had decided she could afford to stay at the shelter full-time for several months before she would need to get another job.

She got in her car and drove home, her thoughts on a long soak and Clayton's unexpected call that morning from Jamaica, asking her to consider coming to spend a long weekend with him there. She frowned, trying to decide how she would spend the next five days, which she could have spent in Jamaica with Clay. The thought of so much time on her hands was rather unsettling. She had managed to keep her heartache at bay by putting in ten to twelve hour-days. Her thoughts turned to Clayton again. Getting over Jeff was proving harder than she'd anticipated. She knew a relationship with Clayton would engage her senses in a way that might finally rid her of her lingering obsession for Jeff. Perhaps she'd been a fool to insist she and Clayton remain friends when they both wanted more.

She usually arrived home at night too tired to do anything but get a quick soak before falling exhausted into bed. When she had time on her hands, her thoughts and her dreams turned to Jefferson and what they might have had. She no longer blamed him exclusively for having taken another woman to his bed. If she had been more understanding of his pain, she wouldn't have issued that ridiculous ultimatum that had ended in his picking up a woman in a bar.

After his pleas that last day in her office, she had expected to have to ignore his phone calls and refuse to see him when he showed up at her condo. He had done neither. She had not seen him since she'd resigned. On her last day at Calder Technologies, he had taken the day off, an action she had considered the final insult.

He had been prepared to marry her and yet he had made no effort to contact her. She knew she was well rid of him, but the ache deep inside persisted, as raw and painful as it had been when that woman had answered his phone in the middle of the night.

She stepped out of the elevator and walked down the hall to her condo. She came to an abrupt stop. Two vases of long-stemmed roses sat outside her apartment door.

More roses from Clayton. Angry tears welled in her eyes. Why couldn't Jefferson be half as romantic and considerate as Clayton? After opening her apartment door and carrying, the vases inside, she reached for the card protruding from the middle of the roses.

When she saw the name scrawled at the bottom of the card, her hands shook. Jefferson.

Forgive me. Please. Jefferson.

CHAPTER TEN

She put the roses on the hall table and leaned her forehead against the door. The sound of the video buzzer made her jump. Her heart raced. She knew it was Jeff. She pressed the buzzer by the door on the intercom. "Yes?"

"It's Jefferson, Sharde. Will you please talk to me?"

Finally. "Yes." She nodded and released the buzzer. When the knock sounded on her door, her heart jumped into her throat.

"Who...who is it?"

"Jefferson."

She took a deep breath and opened the door.

He came in, a bouquet of roses in the crook of one arm. He closed the door, placed the roses on the hall table, and looked at her. "Hi."

She swallowed hard. "Hi."

"How have you been, Sharde?"

"Fine...you?"

"Miserable. I have been absolutely miserable."

"Going through March Madness by yourself was rough, huh?"

He laughed and raked a hand through his hair. "For once Ben was around, but nothing is the same without you."

"So. How are things at the office?"

"Ah...okay. Darbi is doing an adequate job filling in for you." He sighed. "But she's not you, Sharde."

She wet her lips, fighting back tears. "Does she need to be?"

"God, yes! Oh, honey, I miss you. Please tell me you miss me too...just a little."

She pressed a hand against her mouth, shaking her head. Dare she admit how much she missed him? She gulped in a deep breath. "I have."

"Forgive me?" He spread his arms wide.

She walked into his embrace and felt his arms close around her. She buried her face against his shoulder, tears streaming down her cheeks, her body shaking. Holding her close, he sank down to the floor, his lips against her hair. He rocked her, stroking her shoulders. "I'm so sorry I hurt you, honey. So sorry."

She lifted her head and looked up at him through her tears. She touched his face with trembling hands. "It was partly my fault. I knew you were hurt and needed time. I should have been more understanding and given you the time you needed to heal. But I was selfish. I'd waited so long and I wanted you so badly that I pushed you into sleeping with her."

His eyes blazed. "I did not sleep with her, Sharde! I swear I didn't. I took her home because she reminded me of you, but when we got there, I couldn't sleep with her."

"It doesn't matter if you did because—"

"I didn't and it matters to me that you believe me, Sharde."

She looked in his eyes and saw no deception. "I do believe you." She touched his lips. "I'm sorry I was so unreasonable. I should—"

He kissed her fingers. "You weren't unreasonable. You were right. I was trying to make you accountable for past hurts that had nothing to do with you." He stroked his hand over her face, brushing away her tears. "And I was incredibly blind...allowing Linda and Vanessa to make a first-class fool of me while you were right under my nose."

"Why didn't you try to call or see me after I resigned?"

"You were so angry and hurt, I was afraid that if I didn't give you some space I would lose you for good." He reached behind her head, pulling out the pins to allow her hair to fall around her shoulders. He buried his face in the resulting cloud, inhaling deeply. "I thought about you all the time and wanted you so badly I couldn't sleep at night."

He sighed. "Besides, I picked up the phone to call you at least five times every day. And we won't even talk about all the times I drove here in the middle of the night and just sat outside in the parking lot looking up at your dark living room windows. And when I realized you were seeing Frazier—"

"I'm not seeing him!" Well...at least she wasn't seeing him now.

"No? A few weeks ago, one Friday night, I drove by Seafood Wharf and saw you two standing together in the parking lot. He kissed you!"

"On the cheek!"

"He had his hand on the back of your head. I don't think he'd need to do that to kiss your cheek. He was kissing your lips. And you didn't seem to mind!"

She nodded. "He did kiss me on the lips...a few times."

"And you let him?"

She tightened her lips. "Yes, Jefferson, I let him."

"And you enjoyed it?"

"Did you enjoy kissing Vanessa?"

"We're talking about you and Frazier."

"Yes, Jefferson, I enjoyed having him kiss me. And you want to know something? I kissed him back. So where does that leave us?"

He raked his hand through his hair. "I knew I should have put my foot up his ass!"

She laughed. "That's the same thing he wanted to do to you."

He sucked in an angry breath. "And you find this funny?"

"Oh, Jeff, lighten up, will you? If I wanted him instead of you, I could be in Jamaica with him now. We kissed and we both enjoyed it, but we never slept together! We both like seafood and neither of us had any plans, so when he called…"

"How many times have you been out with him?"

"We've shared a couple of lunches and two or three dinners. But we've never slept together."

He nodded. "If I didn't know that, I'd have wrung his over-ly tanned neck by now!"

"He's lonely and so was I and we decided to be friends—without benefits."

"Friends, hell! I saw the way he was looking at you when Ben and I encountered you two that night. He wants far more than friendship from you."

"That's all he got!"

"This *friendship* you have with him. Is it over?"

"He's out of the country at the moment."

"When he returns? Do you plan to see him again?"

She shook her head. "I don't know. I like him. He's fun to be with and easy to talk to."

"If you want to talk to a man other than me, talk to Benton."

She looked at him wondering what he'd say if she told him Benton thought she had a luscious ass. "Are you going to have a problem with my being friends with Clayton?"

"Of course I will!"

"I'm sorry to hear that, Jeff, because I'm not prepared to allow you to pick my friends."

"Meaning what? You're going to go on seeing him no matter what I say?"

"Yes, Jeff. That's exactly what it means."

"So how I feel doesn't matter to you?"

"Of course it does! Why do you think I've kept him at arms' length all these weeks? It was because of you…of how I knew you'd feel and how I feel about *you*. But in that time, he and I have become friends. I'm not prepared to have you walk back into my life and order me to give up his friendship."

"Sharde—"

She shook her head. "Let me finish. I can promise you that we have never slept together and we never will. Is that good enough for you?"

He took a deep breath. "I suppose it will have to be, but—"

"If you ever got to know him, the two of you would like each other."

"Oh, I don't think so. I can't imagine liking a man I *know* is lusting after *my* woman."

"Would you prefer no other man found me attractive?"

"Yes, I would!"

She sighed. "Fine, Jefferson, but I don't want to talk about him. This is about us. I want to talk about us." She moistened her lips. "Did you mean it when you said you'd marry me?"

He nodded. "Yes. That was a lousy way to ask you, but I did mean it." He kissed her cheek. "Tell you what, pack that sweet little red teddy you bought a few months ago and come to the cabin with me. We'll light a fire, have some wine with dinner, and then I'll get down on my knees and I'll ask you again, much more romantically this time."

She swallowed a lump of emotion and frowned at up at

him. "Well, hell, Jefferson, I don't know. You think you can get it right this time?"

He smiled and hugged her close, pressing his cheek against hers. "I know I require a lot of work and—"

"Maybe so, but it seems I'm a glutton for punishment because I'll gladly take you just as you are."

"You will? Really?" He pulled back and looked down at her. "You are so beautiful."

There was a hint of moisture in his eyes and no trace of guile in his voice. He must be blinded by love because she knew he really thought her beautiful.

He stroked her cheek. "Yes, you'll come to the cabin with me, or yes, you'll marry me?"

"Yes…to both…if you're sure…if it's really what you want and not just what you think I want."

He sighed. "I was a fool not to realize before you left how important you were to me. I'm very sure."

She leaned into him. "Jefferson…I love you."

He stared at her, making a sound that was half laugh, half sob, and then he gathered her in his arms and held her so tightly she could barely breathe. She didn't protest. Breathing was overrated. She slipped her arms around his neck, lifting her face to him, offering him her lips, her eternal fidelity, her trust, and her heart.

He pressed his mouth against hers. His kiss was all at once sweet and tender while promising a depth of passion she had missed so much she could barely sleep at night for thinking about it. She surrendered to her desire and love for him, confident her heart would be safe with him. He hadn't actually used the words "I love you," but some things a woman knew without words. The tender passion of his kiss assured her that she was loved. At last, she was Jefferson Calder's woman.

He brushed his lips against hers. She felt the moisture on his cheeks. "I love you too," he whispered. "I'm sorry it took me so long to realize it and even longer to say it."

Yes! Jefferson Calder was in love with her too! Finally, everything was right within her world. She smiled through her tears. "Don't worry. We have the rest of our lives together for you to make it up to me."

He pulled her into a tight embrace. "That's probably not going to be long enough, so I'd better get started now."

She sighed softly as he rained feverish kisses on her neck. "Shall I get out that teddy?"

He lifted his head and unbuttoned her blouse. Removing her bra, he brushed his lips against her nipples. A shock of desire shot down her spine to curl her toes. "Oh!"

He lifted his head and quickly undressed them both. When they stood naked, he cupped her face between his palms. "Save it for another time. I'm so hungry for you I don't want anything between us..."

She stroked a hand down his chest, loving the feel of his tight abs. "Nothing? Not even a condom?"

"The only thing going into your sweet pussy tonight is my bare cock."

She sucked in a breath. If he wasn't going to at least make a token argument for their using a condom, he really was committed to her. "Oh, Jeff! I've been a bad girl," she told him. "I think I need to be spanked."

"I think so too." Slipping one arm around her waist to hold her tight so she could feel his hard cock between their bodies, he lifted his other hand and gave each of her cheeks a light paddling.

With her heart racing in anticipation of the night ahead of them, he took her hand in his and led her to her bedroom.

He bent her over the chair by the window. She closed her eyes, certain he was about to fuck her ass. Instead, he kissed his way down her back to her cheeks. He pressed several warm, biting caresses against her bottom, then sat in the chair, stretched her over his knees, and spanked her until she gasped and shuddered each time his palm landed on her cheeks.

Then, when her ass stung and she was breathless with need, he took her to the bed. He placed her on her hands and knees. Moments later he kneeled behind her. He kissed her cheeks again, and then gently parted them.

She caught her breath and looked back at him. A condom covered his cock and he held a tube of lube in his hand. "What…are you going to do with that?"

"What do you think?" He lightly lubed the condom and then, holding her cheeks apart, he used a finger to press some of the warm liquid inside her. The muscles of her stomach tightened as his finger pierced her, pushing the lube into her. He added a second finger and gently pumped into her.

"Oh, baby, you're so tight. This is going to be good."

"Jefferson, I didn't say I was going to let you—"

"I don't recall asking for permission." He removed his fingers, parted her cheeks again, and placed his cock between her cheeks at her backdoor. "You've been a bad girl and bad girls get fucked up their pretty brown asses."

She tensed, feeling him hard and warm against her. "I don't think I'm ready for this."

"Then why are you trembling? And don't expect me to believe you're trembling in fear." He slapped both her cheeks. "It's time you learned who the hell you belong to, Sharde."

"Jeff—"

"Save it," he said and propelled his hips forward.

She caught her breath and closed her eyes as the head of his cock lodged in her. He paused, allowing her to catch her breath. He bent over her, brushing his warm lips against her shoulders. "All right?"

All right? The man she loved was about to make one of her fantasies come true. "Yes."

"Then here I come, baby." Sliding his hands up to her hips, he held her still and slowly pushed his hips forward.

She moaned as inch by inch his big cock slipped into her rectum and up into her eager ass. With half his cock inside her, she gasped. She so was full she was afraid to move. "That's enough," she whispered.

"It's not nearly enough," he said in a hoarse voice. "You belong to me and after tonight, there won't be any doubt of that." Sliding one arm around her waist and keeping his cock in her, he rolled onto his side, pulling her down with him. Lying on his side behind her, he pushed his hips forward.

"Oh...god!" She cried out as the rest of his cock shot up into her ass. "Jeff! Oh, my god, Jeff!"

Balls deep in her, he put the hand he'd used to finger her ass over her breasts. The fingers of the other hand slid around her body to her pussy. "Now," he groaned, his lips against her neck. "You're all mine and it's time for pretty bad girls to get punished."

With an ass full of cock and a wet pussy, she did the only thing she could. She surrendered to him completely, driving her hips back against his body and reaching one hand behind to clutch at his buttocks as he started to fuck her ass. "Oh, yes! Punish me, Jeff!"

He eased most of his cock out of her and stroked half his length back into her. He did that a few times as he nibbled at her neck. His first sweet strokes in and out of her were long and shallow. "How does this feel?"

"It hurts." But even as she spoke, she thrust her hips back against him and moaned in delight as she felt his cock sliding up into her to reclaim her ass.

He laughed and moved his thumb to press against her clit. "It's about to hurt even more. I have to punish you until you realize who you belong to."

She wiggled her hips against him. "Oh, baby, punish me!"

"Punishment coming up," he promised, his voice low and barely audible. Rotating his hips, he pushed forward again. This time instead of withdrawing when he was halfway inside her, he kept pushing until she felt his pubic hair against her cheeks.

"Hmmm," she moaned, her ass stretching to accommodate his cock.

He held still for a moment, finger fucking her pussy and rubbing her clit. Then as she enjoyed those wonderful sensations, he moved again, withdrawing and then driving his entire length back into her.

"Ooooh!" She moaned as he withdrew and shot back into her with more force. "That hurts!"

"That's the price you pay for having such a sweet, tight ass, baby," he groaned, bit her shoulder, and began thrusting into her with deep, powerful strokes that sent waves of pleasure tinged with pain through her.

She moaned, then gasped, and arched her back, as he propelled his cock deep in her ass with hard, piston-like strokes.

She lost her ability to think. Her entire world revolved around her ass and the big dick pummeling it with such a fierce, hungry passion. A wall of pain crashed over her when he rolled her onto her stomach, pressed his weight onto her back, and fucked her ass in a fury.

Sobbing with pain, her thighs quivered each time he shot his cock balls deep in her ass. Lost in a world where pain and pleasure intermingled and fought for dominance with each other, her toes curled, and her pussy gushed as she experienced the most powerful orgasm of her life.

It battered her in torrents, leaving her feeling weak and dazed as she suffered through several glorious aftershocks. When her senses returned, she heard him groan. He slammed his hips against hers and came.

He collapsed against her back, his big, damp body shaking. He lay with his mouth pressed against her neck for several moments before he finally eased out of her.

She moaned in pain as he did and then collapsed in his arms when he reached for her.

He kissed her forehead and held her. "I'm so sorry, baby. I know I hurt you, but I—"

"You meant to hurt me," she told him. "Don't bother denying it."

His hands stilled on her back. "Okay, I won't."

She pulled away from him and bolted into a sitting position. "You have the nerve to admit it?"

He sighed and sat up. He pulled her against him as they sat against her headboard. "Yes, I admit I wanted to hurt you. . .but just a little. Given the tightness of your ass and the size of my cock, it was a given some pain was going to be involved."

"And that was okay with you?"

"Yes, but only because I knew you were enjoying it. Otherwise, I would have been gentler." He palmed her cheek and turned her to face him. "And you did enjoy it. Didn't you?"

How could she deny it with her pussy even now filling with fresh moisture as she thought of a repeat performance? "Maybe a little."

He laughed and kissed her. "You squealed like a stuck pig," he teased. "You enjoyed it more than a little. You like having your big ass spanked and fucked. Where the hell have you been all my life?"

"Right under your nose, you bonehead!"

"Speaking of boneheads..." He waved his cock at her.

She laughed and collapsed in his arms. "Oh, Jeff. Is this real?"

He slid down on the bed, taking her with him. He gently cupped her burning ass. "Oh, yeah, baby. It's real."

"And you love me as much as I love you?"

"No. I love you more." He cupped her face and stared down at her. "Never doubt that. I plan to spend the next...oh...fifty or sixty years making sure you know how much I love you."

They cuddled for awhile, and then went to take a bath together. When they returned to bed, she wanted him again. She rolled onto her back and parted her legs in a wanton invitation.

"You are so beautiful, Sharde." He stroked his hands up and down her thighs before gently stroking two fingers inside her. "Hmmm. Looks like someone has been a bad girl and needs to be punished."

She lifted her hips off the bed. "Oh, hell yeah, baby, punish me!"

Smiling, he climbed onto the bed, settling between her legs. As she felt the big head of his dick slowly taking possession of her aching pussy, inch by delicious inch, she moaned, closed her eyes, and lost herself in him.

The End

Following is an excerpt from the upcoming sequel to Falling For Sharde, Nice Girls Do. Nice Girls do is the second book in the Taking Chances series, published by Loose-id (http://www.loose-id.net).

NICE GIRLS DO
By
Marilyn Lee

The moment Clayton Frazier spotted Sharde Donovan standing in the airport terminal, what felt like a silly grin spread across his face. Having spent most of the plane ride from Florida to Philadelphia thinking about her, he felt almost as if he'd conjured her up. Quickening his pace, he reached her in moments. "Hi, honey!"

"Hi, Clay."

He caressed her cheek. "Why didn't you tell me you were meeting me?"

"I wanted to surprise you."

The smile that warmed her smooth, brown face didn't quite reach her dark eyes. Some of his delight dissipated. "Well, you've done that. Now tell me, am I going to like the reason you chose to surprise me?"

She caught his hand and leaned up to kiss him-on the damn cheek. "Welcome back, Clay."

Recalling the taste of her full lips as she passionately returned his kisses the last time they'd seen each other several weeks earlier, her chaste kiss did not bode well for his hopes of their becoming friends with benefits.

The carryon bag hanging off his shoulder suddenly felt as if it weighed a couple of hundred pounds. Allowing the carryon to fall to the floor, he drew her into his arms.

She pressed her hands against his shoulders, turning her head to avoid his lips. "We need to talk, Clay."

He glanced down at her left hand. A diamond solitaire winked at him from her third finger. He released her. "Oh, shit, Sharde! You're going to marry the bonehead?"

She nodded. "Yes."

"Why?"

"I love him." She reached for his hand and squeezed it. "I know you're disappointed, but please try to be happy for me, Clay."

The woman he'd wanted for himself was telling him she was going to marry a bonehead and he was supposed to be happy about it? He pulled his hand away from her and picked up his carryon. "He doesn't deserve you."

"Clay. Please." She reached for his hand again. "I know you believe that, but I love him."

"Does he love you?"

A radiant smile spread across her face and this time it reached her eyes. She nodded, squeezing his hand. "Oh, yes, Clay. He does. Isn't it wonderful?"

Looking into her dark eyes, aglow with happiness, he knew he was looking at the one that got away. Instead of pursuing her with the goal of landing her in his bed as his significant other, he had tried to play nice and be her friend first. And look where playing nice had landed him-he'd lost a woman he'd been a breath of away from falling in love with.

He narrowed his gaze. Whoever had said nice guys finished

last, had known just what the hell he was talking about. No more Mr. Nice Guy for him. The next time he met a woman he wanted-he was going to pursue her until she ended up in his bed. No more of this friends first shit.

She tugged at his hand. "Clay? Can we still be friends?"

He's spent the last five weeks horny and celibate because he wanted to be able to tell her he hadn't been with anyone while he'd been visiting his parents in Jamaica. She'd clearly not been celibate and now she wanted to be friends? How the hell was he supposed to be friends with a woman he wanted so much he'd passed up countless opportunities to bed other women because none of them were her?

"Clay? Please?"

He wanted a shower, a drink, and lots of pussy...from her. Besides, he already had one female friend. He raked a hand through his hair and pasted a smile on his face. "Friends, huh? With or without benefits?"

She gave him a cool, reproving stare. "Clay!"

He arched a brow. "I guess that's a without, huh?"

She nodded firmly.

He sighed. "Fine, but you tell that lucky boneheaded bastard that he'd better treat you right this time or I'll plant my size twelve foot so far up his ass, he'll—"

"Clay! Jeff and I have settled our differences. We're happy and in love. Can't you be happy for us?"

"Why the hell should I be happy for him?"

"For me then?"

He touched her cheek. "I wanted you for myself."

He watched a hint of rose stain her cheeks. She nodded. "I know and if it's any consolation, I wanted you too. You'll never know how close I came to..."

"And now you think we can be friends?"

"I know it won't be easy…but I…I thought if we both wanted it…"

"And bonehead is okay with this idea of our being friends?"

She grimaced and shook her head. "Not really."

"Really?" He grinned at her. "Then I'm all for anything that makes bonehead unhappy."

"Clay! His name is Jefferson."

"Whatever." He frowned. "Damn, Sharde. Are you sure you want to marry him?"

She nodded. "I'm very sure and very happy."

Damn it, but she did look happy. He nodded and bent to kiss her cheek. "Then congratulations and best wishes."

She hugged him, pressing her lips against the corner of his mouth. "Thanks, Clay." She drew back to stare up at him. "I know you're not happy, but you're not hurt…are you? I'd hate to think I did anything to mislead you or hurt you in any way. If I did, I'm so sorry."

He'd known from the moment he first asked her out that she was probably in love with his chief business rival Jefferson Calder. "There's no need for sorrow or regret on your part, Sharde. You've always been honest about your feelings for old bone-Calder. I'm a little more than disappointed at the moment, but I'm a big boy. I'll get over it."

He stroked her cheek. "Now. Do you come bearing a car or are we going to need a cab? Or is he waiting to snatch you away the moment you're finished delivering the bad news?"

"I drove here alone. I was hoping I could give you a lift."

If he had a quarter of the sense God gave him, he'd say goodbye to her, walk away, and never look back. "Sure. Let me get my bags."

"Okay." She gave him a relieved smiled. "I'll go get the car and meet you outside."

"Okay." He watched her until she disappeared from sight before he went to pick up his luggage. *I hope you know what the hell you're doing trying to be friends with her, Clayton.*

Twenty minutes later, as they drove away from the airport, Sharde dropped her second bombshell. "Do you have any plans for this afternoon, Clay?"

He resisted the urge to tell her he'd planned to spend the afternoon fucking her. He kept his gaze on the highway ahead. "No. I'm just going to shower, have a drink, and relax. Why?"

"No reason."

"No reason?" He glanced at her profile before turning his gaze back to the highway. "I doubt that. Why are you interested in what I'm doing this afternoon?"

"No real reason. I just thought..."

He waited several moments before he spoke again. "Yes? You thought?"

"Well, I know you like black women..."

That was putting it mildly. He'd always preferred black women, especially after his first night with his best friend Cami. "And?"

"And I have a friend who just happens to be black, gorgeous, and single."

His lips tightened. "What's the matter, Sharde? Feeling so guilty for kicking my ass to the curb you now feel sorry and want to fix me up with your friend?"

She made a small, distressed sound. "Oh, Clay! I'm sorry. I—"

He shook his head and turned to look at her. "No! You have no reason to be sorry. I'm the one who should be sorry for being a jackass. You never lied to or deceived me."

She cast a quick look at him. "I am sorry, Clay."

"Don't be. You have a right to be happy without thinking it's at my expense. I'm just so damned grouchy because I'm horny as hell. I need some pussy." He arched a brow. "I don't suppose you're feeling sorry enough to give me some, are you?"

"Clayton! No!"

Watching the hint of color rush to her cheek, he laughed and patted her thigh. "Don't have a stroke. I was just teasing... and testing your resolve."

"It's very solid."

"Lucky bonehead."

"Clay—"

"Yes. I know. His name is Jefferson."

She nodded, her shoulders relaxing. "So about this friend of mine. She's divorced and not interested in anything serious right now."

"And?"

"And she wouldn't be averse to a strictly sexual relationship."

"Really? Well I'll keep her in mind."

"Don't you want to meet her? She'll be going away on a business trip soon, but I can probably get you two together this afternoon."

Her persistence surprised him. She really must feel guilty. "And this black, gorgeous friend of yours dates white men?"

"Well...not exactly, but I'm sure Darbi would go out with you if you asked her."

"At the moment, I want sex, not a date. And I have no interest or inclination to waste time and energy pursuing a woman who doesn't date white men."

"I admit you might have to do a little chasing, but she'd be worth the effort."

"Hmmm."

"I wish you'd reconsider, Clay."

"Why?"

"I know the two of you could be good together. She's very nice."

"Really? Well, as I said, I'm not that interested in dating a nice girl who doesn't. I'm more interested in a not so nice girl who does."

"There are some nice girls who do, Clay and Darbi has a lot of..."

"What? Problems? Lovers? What?"

She shook her head. "I can't say more without revealing her confidence, but I know the two of you would be great together."

"And this Darbi is..."

"Darbi Raymond."

"She works for bonehead?"

"Clay!"

He smiled. "Calder. That better?"

"Yes and she's very nice."

"Listen, I appreciate your concern, but I really am capable of landing my own lovers."

"I know, but I just hate the thought of you being sexually frustrated."

"You hate it? Imagine how I feel."

Her lips twitched and she laughed. After a moment, he joined in.

"So can I introduce you two?"

"No."

She sighed. "If you change your mind, Clay, I—"

"Drop it, Sharde."

"Fine."

Still smiling, he settled back in his seat and closed his eyes. Once he'd had some pussy he'd be more inclined to view her reconciliation with Calder in a less tragic light. Maybe then the two of them could be friends. But first things first. He needed to see Cami. As selfish as it was, he hoped she was between lovers at the moment.

Forty-five minutes later, after sweeping Sharde into his arms and pressing a long, last, greedy kiss against her sweet lips, he said good-bye to her, and walked into his center city condo. Noting the message indictor on the answering machine in the front hall blinking, he sighed. He had four messages.

He decided the messages could wait, but a shower couldn't. In the master bedroom of his three-bedroom condo, he kicked off his shoes. The phone rang. Ignoring it, he sat down to remove his socks. Rising he removed the rest of his clothes as listened to his answering machine greeting.

Hi. I'm not home. Leave a message.

He was at the door of the adjourning bathroom when he heard his mother's frantic voice.

"Clayton? Clayton, if you're home, please pick up. Clayton, please! This is important."

Frowning, he quickly crossed the bedroom to pick up the cordless phone on his night table. "Mom? What's wrong?"

"Oh, thank God, I got you, Clayton."

"What's wrong, Mom?"

"It's Amber. You have to talk to her, Clayton."

Amber. He'd noticed a marked and unpleasant change in her during his visit to Jamaica. He sighed and sat on the side of his bed. "Who does she owe money to now?"

"I wish it was just a case of her owing money. This time she's gotten herself in a big mess. You'd better sit down, Clayton."

Shit. Just wanted he needed-bailing Amber out of another damned mess. "What's going on, Mom?"

"She wasn't happy when I insisted she had to go to the states. She'll be staying with you until we can figure out how to handle this."

"Handle what? And why can't she stay with Damien?"

"She needs her big brother now more than ever, Clayton."

He frowned, annoyed by the censure he heard in her voice. "Damien's her big brother too."

"Yes, but he doesn't have a spare bedroom."

Lucky bastard. No spare bedroom meant not having to take Amber in when she got herself into yet another mess that his mother couldn't deal with and Xavier refused to admit was a problem.

"Besides, he has no patience. He seems to forget the messes he had to be bailed out of. Don't get me started on your brother's selfish streak, Clayton."

He raked a hand through his hair, recalling the good old days when he'd been an only child. Amber would be starting Harvard in September. She'd want to spend at least a month shopping for new clothes so he'd only have her in his hair for two months or so.

"When is she arriving, Mom, and what's wrong?"

***

After calming his mother down, he called Cami. "Hi, honey. It's Clay."

A woman with a warm, island voice answered. "Clayton! How lovely to hear from you. How are you?"

"So-so. You?"

"Fairly well. How is the family…your parents…Amber… Damien?"

"Amber is Amber, but everyone else is fine. Your family?"

"Great."

"Good. Are you free this afternoon?"

"I'm always free to spend a few hours with you, Clay. Come whenever you like."

"Can I bring you anything?"

She hesitated. "Is Damien seeing anyone?"

"I don't think so. Why do you ask?"

"No special reason. I was just wondering. I haven't seen him in a while."

"He's had his hands full keeping Fra-Tech on track while I've been in Jamaica."

"Of course."

"So, do you need me to bring anything?"

"Just bring that big, hard dick of yours. I'll supply lots of condoms, the lube, the warm, wet, willing pussy, and the tight ass."

He felt a surge of lust, tempered by affection. He loved that Cami never played games or pretended not to enjoy sex. On his sixteenth birthday, the eighteen-year old Cami had given him his first taste of brown sugar. After a hot, two year love affair, they'd decided they were not in love and become friends. During the last fifteen years, they'd developed a closer friendship with occasional benefits.

He fondled his cock. "You're making me hot."

She laughed. "Don't play with yourself, Clay. Save your lust for me."

He laughed and released his cock. "I'll see you soon."

"I'll be waiting, Clay."

Nice Girls Do—coming from Loose-id (http://www. loose-id.com).